To Kerrie
Thanks for your support with the series!

Starting Over With the Billionaire

In the Name of Love Book 3

Wynter Wilde

With love,
Wynter

For all who have felt loss, there is always hope that we can heal...

Copyright © 2024 by Wynter Wilde

All rights reserved.

No part of this book may be reproduced in any form or by any electronic or mechanical means, including information storage and retrieval systems, without written permission from the author, except for the use of brief quotations in a book review.

 Created with Vellum

Author Note

Please be aware that this story includes references to grief and loss of a spouse, as well as historical childhood neglect, which some readers may find emotional.

Starting Over With the Billionaire – In the Name of Love Book 3

Lucas Barrett: I've a head for business and a body for... well, having a good time. By day, I rule the boardroom. By night, I rule the bedroom. The women I date have no expectations of me and I have none of them. Any hint of one of them wanting more and that's the last they'll see of me.

Carla Russell: After over a decade in New York, I've returned to London. It's not what I wanted but sometimes life doesn't work out the way we planned. I fell in love, got married and we talked about starting a family, but tragedy struck and my world fell apart. All I'm certain about now is that I gave my heart once and I know I'll never love again.

Lucas: When I bump into a school friend's younger sister at a bar, I consider hitting on her but there's something in her eyes that warns me not to even try. Instead, I find myself offering her a place to stay until she can get back on her feet.

Carla: Staying at the luxury city apartment of my older brother's friend was not part of the plan but when I meet him at a bar, I find I'm curious. He was an obnoxious teenager and I used to hate his guts but now he's all grown up and undeniably hot. Plus, it's the coldest winter in years, I have nowhere else to go because the hotels are all full and there's a snowstorm on the way.

Will Carla find a way to start over with the billionaire or will she leave him behind as the snow begins to melt?

PROLOGUE – Carla Russell – 10 months earlier

There are moments in life that we barely notice as we float languidly through them like dust motes on sun warmed air. These moments are the ones we think don't matter at the time, the ones we don't need to take heed of as we look forward to times that will hold significance for us. But these are the moments we should treasure most, the ones where we wake with a beloved partner sleeping next to us in the bed we share, shopping at the grocery store for a low-sugar granola we both like, lifting two toothbrushes as we clean around the sink. I've been guilty of taking these moments for granted, of daydreaming about the big house we'll have when we can afford it with a white picket fence in a quiet neighbourhood; of being able to buy organic ingredients to make my own granola when I have the time and money; and about how nice it would be if my partner thought to clean the sink once in a while without being asked to do so. If only I'd known what lay ahead, then I'd have treasured those times, held them close and never let them go.

Of course, that's not possible. Nothing lasts forever, and we can't make time stand still, no matter how much we might want to freeze it. One minute we have a life to treasure and the next we have a life we didn't want and didn't choose. We cannot see past the pain that's filling us up and eating us from the inside like a rat trapped inside a watermelon trying to gnaw its way out. Because that's how it feels, like the pain gnaws, gnaws, gnaws. Nothing takes it away — not exercise, alcohol, prescription drugs or sleep, because even if they temporarily ease the pain, it returns with a vengeance that leaves us breathless.

Two weeks have passed since my normal, simple life was turned upside down, and everything I knew was ripped away from me. The reality, the security, and the predictability of my life vanished in a split second one morning when I woke from a deep sleep, and I know the world will never look the same again. The life I had will never be mine again. Everything I had is no longer mine.

I am lost and I don't think I will ever be found...

Chapter 1

Carla Russell

As the plane descends over a dull, grey London, I tug my thick cardigan tighter over my chest and huddle into my seat. The belt presses uncomfortably against my lap and my feet in their scuffed boots are firmly planted on the floor in front of me. Take-off and landing are the worst things about flying. I can cope when I'm in the air and feel a sense of equilibrium, but the plane rising into the air and descending towards the ground both fill me with unease. I've read the statistics and apparently the chances of dying in a plane crash are something like one in 11 million, and the odds of drowning in the bath or being killed by lightning are far more likely. There were other facts I read too when I looked into this, but for me, being in a plane brings a tremendous sense of vulnerability and flying is not something I enjoy. This is, of course, one of the reasons why I've rarely flown over the past decade, as well as the fact that I was happy where I was and with my life, so I felt no need to hop on a plane and head back to good old Blighty. But now ... things have changed and the life I loved in New York is no longer filled with joy. Where once I felt fulfilled, excited, and that I belonged, I now feel rudderless, lost and confused, empty and alien. With Christmas approaching, the first without the life I held so dear, I couldn't bear to stay another month, so I gave notice on the furnished one-bedroom apartment, sold what I couldn't pack in a suitcase, and booked my flight home.

Home...

Am I heading home? I grew up in Topsham in Exeter, a scenic and historic estuary port with a rich maritime history. I had a happy childhood living with my calm, loving, and sensible parents and my protective older brother. Apart from losing my grandparents when I was in my teens, there were no great traumas, and life was good. Perhaps that was why I had the confidence to travel alone to America to work with an international children's charity. My parents had raised me to believe I could be anything I aspired to be and I decided I wanted to dedicate my life to helping others. I could follow in the footsteps of those who'd gone before me, live alone in a different country and create a new life for myself there, then, when the time was right, I'd move on again. But it turned out that the salary the charity paid me wasn't great, and life in New York wasn't cheap, so I had to take on extra work cleaning hotel rooms. Despite all this, I was happy because I had *him*, and he always made me feel that anything was possible.

My stomach flips over as the plane descends, clouds caressing the windows like wet cotton wool, the ground creeping closer by the second. My knuckles are white from gripping the seat handles so tightly, and I have to remind myself to breathe and lower my shoulders. No sense of calm ever came from keeping your shoulders up around your ears and holding your breath, for fuck's sake.

The word *home* pops into my mind again. Home is where the heart is, right?

And where is my heart?

In ashes.

Floating around Central Park, spread out on the breeze and carried far away, just like he wanted. He didn't get to see all the places he wanted to see, to do all the things he longed to do, but by being cremated and having his ashes scattered, I hoped he'd be able to do so after his death.

My best friend.

My lover.

My husband.

My heart.

I have left my heart in Manhattan, and I don't think I'll ever get it back.

Chapter 2

Lucas Barrett

I've a head for business and a body for what my dear old Catholic grandmother would have called sin. If she was alive now, I would be tempted to tell her that if sex is sin, then sin feels good and, based on my romantic history, I have been one big, bad sinner.

After a day of meetings, I'm tired and tense. With Christmas approaching, Cavendish Construction is busy with planning and preparation for the new year and beyond. January can be a slow month as people recover from Christmas indulgence and it's like they have to rev themselves up again to get going. If it was up to me, I'd scrap the holidays and keep the momentum going all year round. You can take a break when you've earned it and not just because the calendar says so. We'd save so much money if I could just introduce this concept for once, but whenever I've raised it, Edward and Jack haven't wanted to know. The best thing about Christmas, as far as I'm concerned, is groups of drunk women out looking for a festive fling, and when I'm really lucky, I might get two for the price of one underneath the mistletoe.

I'm keen to hit the gym and work out some of this frustration. I might even get a massage from Letitia at the luxury spa that's part of the health club. She's a pretty little thing, and she offers discreet extras to her favourite clients. The first time she asked if I'd like *the special*, I was expecting her to dig her elbows into the knots in my lower back, but then she rolled me over and slipped her hand under the towel. Suffice it to say, I was a lot more relaxed after she'd finished. And it's not even *that kind* of spa where you'd expect to be offered a happy ending, but sometimes, the employees at these places like to go the extra mile. Who am I to deny them job satisfaction? Of course, I'm not a monster; I repaid the favour by lifting her onto the massage table, peeling off her trousers and panties, then eating her sweet little pussy until she hit the peak of her own stress relief. Since then, every time I book a massage, she's waiting for me with a seductive smile and no underwear at all beneath those fitted white scrubs.

'You heading to the gym?' Edward Cavendish asks as we board the lift together. There's a gym in the office building, but I like to head to the health club in Mayfair. It has a two-year waiting list and the clientele are wealthy, ranging from celebrities to royalty to billionaires, and we all want privacy from prying eyes.

'I am.' Stretching my neck from side to side, I say, 'I need a massage.'

Edward glances sideways at me and his eyebrows lift a fraction. 'It's like that, is it?'

I laugh. He knows me too well.

'It's all right for you married men,' I say, referring to him and our friend and colleague, Jack Kendrick, who got married earlier this year in Vegas. 'You get sex on tap, but single men like me have to go looking for it.'

Edward shakes his head and I hear a grumble deep in his chest. Seems like I've woken the beast.

'Marriage is not about *sex on tap*, Lucas,' he says quietly, but there's a chill in his tone. 'Marriage is about love, loyalty, and commitment to one person. It's about respecting that person and I'd like you to remember that.'

I clear my throat, aware that I don't want to overstep the line. Edward is one of my best friends and he's been through a lot over the years. The last thing I want to do is to offend him. I love the man like a brother.

'No offence meant, Ed. You know I'm fooling around.'

The lift stops at the ground floor and the doors slide open. Edward places a hand over the one to keep it open, then he turns to me and grins.

'I know that, Lucas. But Ava's my wife and I don't see her as an object. Although my body burns with passion for her, my heart is filled with love and respect, and I will never reduce her to a mere sexual object.'

'All right, Mr Darcy, keep your top hat on.'

We stare at each other for a few seconds, the air between us taught with friction, and then Edward's mouth twitches and he laughs. I join him and we're still laughing as we exit the lift and cross the lobby floor.

'I really didn't mean to speak out of line,' I say when we stop before the glass doors that open out onto the street.

Edward looks out at the cold, grey day beyond the glass, then he turns back to me and nods. 'I can't wait until you fall in love, Lucas, because perhaps then you'll understand what I'm talking about.'

'I'm never falling for anyone.' Shaking my head, I smile. 'Love and me, we're not suited.'

'We'll see.' He cocks his right eyebrow in challenge. 'We will see.'

He pats me on the shoulder and we leave the building together, the icy December wind swirling around us as if to remind us it's winter in London and Christmas is on the way.

Chapter 3

Carla

It took me ages to get through passport control and then to collect my suitcase from baggage reclaim. By the time I got outside the airport, the coaches running directly to Central London were full. I tried the Uber app but had no joy there and ended up waiting in the queue for a taxi. Apparently, the weather report isn't good and everyone's rushing to get home or booking into hotels. I thought I'd booked a cheap room in London but when I checked, the booking had failed, and then I remembered that I'd cancelled the credit card I'd tried to use. I'm sure it will be fine though, so now that I'm inside the warmth of a taxi, I'll try again. There must be something available.

My plan is to stay at a hotel for the night, then make my way back to Exeter tomorrow. Or that was my intention, as bad weather can severely disrupt British transport. Knowing my luck, the trains will be cancelled and I'll be stuck in London for a few days. Having said that, it's been years since I spent any time in London so it might be a nice way of acclimatising to being back in the UK. After all, I'm planning on moving back in with Mum and Dad for a while, so before I head back to Exeter, perhaps I should enjoy what London has to offer.

'Dammit!' I slam my phone down on the seat next to me.

'What's wrong, love?' The chirpy taxi driver glances at me in the rear-view mirror.

'I can't find a hotel room.'

He chuckles, then replies in his rich Cockney accent, 'It's December in London, love. Everyone's here for the Christmas lights and shopping, as well as the shows. You should have booked in advance.'

Swallowing my sharp retort of *I thought I had booked a room, cheers, cabby,* I gaze out of the window. Was that a flake of snow? Scowling at the sky, my stomach lurches. At the moment white flakes are drifting down, but I know from experience that things can change rapidly around here.

When we reach Central London, the traffic slows right down to a crawl and I choke back a sigh. I've been here so many times in the past, but it all seems so strange now. Familiar landmarks appear less impressive compared to those I've become accustomed to in Manhattan. Everything feels surreal and the uncomfortable tightening starts in my chest, a sensation like I'm being squeezed by a boa constrictor and I'm not going to be able to cling to consciousness.

Breathe slowly, Carla.

The voice whispers into my ear, and I look around.

'Kofi?' His name escapes my lips.

'What's that, love?' the driver asks.

'Nothing.' Lowering my gaze to my lap, I press my hands together, gripping tight.

Kofi was always so good with me when my anxiety rose. I didn't suffer from it growing up, but the big move to New York, the cost of living, as well as the pandemic and how it affected daily life, all contributed to my condition. Kofi knew how to help me, though. He'd simply hug me tight, stroke my hair and tell me it would all be fine. Even when our bills weren't paid or we had to have pasta again for dinner, he never once made me feel bad about things. I worked the two jobs, of course, but for minimum wage, and with his meagre teacher's salary, we didn't have cash to spare. But we had each other and our love, and that was what mattered.

A tear escapes my right eye and trickles down my cheek and I brush at it absently. Over the past ten months I've cried so many tears, sobbed until my throat was raw and my voice hoarse. And what did it achieve? Where did it get me? Nowhere. It gave me a headache and exhausted me, left me needing to lie down in a dark bedroom and sleep. Escaping into sleep always seems like the only choice I have. The worst thing about sleeping though, is that on waking up, I have to grieve all over again.

'Where are you wanting to be dropped then, love?' the taxi driver asks.

'I don't mind,' I say. 'Actually, drop me somewhere I can get a drink.'

'A proper drink, love?' He meets my eyes again in the mirror.

'Yes. A proper drink.'

I know that alcohol will only offer a temporary numbness, but right now, I'm at a loss as to what I'm going to do. Tiredness has blurred my edges and I can barely think straight. A drink might help to warm me up and sharpen my mind, or at least allow me a chance to think about what the hell I'm going to do. I'm guessing I'll need to take a train somewhere to find a hotel out of the city and stay there instead. It's not what I wanted, but I'm beyond hoping that things will work out as I want. It seems that the universe just doesn't have good things in store for me, either that or someone has made a voodoo doll of me and is casting spells over it. Why they'd do that, I have no idea, but I watch a lot of true crime TV and know that it doesn't take much to piss people off these days. I actually found a Ouija board once underneath a duvet in a hotel room I was cleaning, and next to it was a strap-on dildo and a used condom. There was no way I was going to change that bed and get accused of moving the guest's *belongings*, so I shook out the quilt over them then sprayed some air freshener around the room. Perhaps it was the owner of the Ouija board who cursed me because they realised I'd seen beneath that duvet.

Sliding a hand down my face, I sigh inwardly. I'm so tired now that I'm thinking nonsense thoughts and I really need to sleep. Jet lag will no doubt kick in soon too and I'll have to crawl into a shop doorway and sleep there.

Life could have been so different if Kofi was still here and I can't help wishing with every fibre of my being that he was. But I know that all the wishing in the world won't change what happened. All I can do now is take a deep breath and keep moving forwards.

Whether I want to or not.

What I do know is that Kofi would want me to keep going. We loved each other so very much and he always wanted the best for me. The problem is, I no longer know what that means and can't ask him to find out.

Chapter 4
Lucas

Turns out I didn't want a hand job from the masseuse after all. She looked cute this evening but when it came down to it, I just wasn't in the mood. I told her I was tired and needed my neck and shoulders massaged and she seemed miffed but then perhaps she was feeling horny and hoping for some attention herself.

After my massage I showered, then headed home to my apartment to change and now I'm walking through Covent Garden admiring the lights and decorations. Don't get me wrong, I'm not a big Christmas fan at all, but I'm also not immune to a pretty setting and Covent Garden is outstanding.

It's busy with tourists and shoppers as well as workers heading home or off to their evening shifts. There's snow in the air and falling snowflakes catch the light as they drift down and sparkle like diamonds. It makes me pause in front of the 60ft tall Christmas tree and admire the 30,000 lights and giant baubles that adorn its branches. I'm not sure if it's my age or the time of year, but now and then, at moments like this, I think it might be nice to turn to a special someone and say, 'Isn't it beautiful?'

Laughing, I shake that silly thought away. A special someone would put demands on me and my time, then drain me emotionally and probably financially. A special someone would need love and tenderness, respect, and loyalty, and not someone as dark and broken inside as me. I'm better off being single. I can eat, sleep and fuck where I like, and never have to worry about how I'm affecting someone else's happiness.

Deciding that a vodka martini is in order, I make my way to a cocktail bar that opened recently after a full refurbishment of the premises, and step inside to be greeted by warm air laced with aromas of cinnamon and cloves. It seems that the mulled wine is popular tonight.

At the bar, I order my drink and while I wait, I lean against the bar and look around. People sit at tables and perch on bar stools, talking to friends and colleagues. Others stare at their mobile phones, the light from the screens casting a blue glow on their skin and making them appear alien or otherworldly. Some stand in groups, talking and laughing, sipping colourful cocktails or glasses of wine as they share details of their weeks, most likely bragging about achievements or slagging off micromanagers. Women tower in heels and flick long hair over bare shoulders while men nod attentively and try to pretend they're not thinking about getting the women home for some night-time adventures.

The mixologist places my drink on the bar, and I nod my thanks then take a sip. It's strong and exactly how I like it with one olive. When I turn back to look out at the room, the door opens and a woman wearing a black faux fur coat and bobble hat steps inside. As is my nature, I scan her to gauge her attractiveness and note the leather gloves and rather battered brown boots. She's dragging a large suitcase that could house a small family and it looks like she's struggling to pull it over the doorstep. There's snow on her hat and coat and her nose is red from the cold. Something inside me steps up and before I know what I'm doing, I abandon my martini and dash across the room to her aid.

'Hey there. Can I help you?' I ask, offering my hands in a show of helpfulness or as a gesture to show I mean no harm. After all, I can't just grab the suitcase if she doesn't want my help, can I?

She looks up at me and I'm staring into pearly grey eyes framed by shapely ginger brows. Her nose is even redder from here and her cheeks are pink. Up close, I can see that she has hair sticking to her cheeks and her neck from where the wind must have thrown the snow at her.

'Oh ... uhhh ... thanks.' She blinks once, twice then releases the handle of the suitcase, so I take hold of it and pull it towards me.

'You look frozen,' I say, feeling an urge to hug her to me and warm her up, but knowing that would seem weird because we've only just met, and I don't even know her name. 'Follow me.'

I lead the way through the bar towards the room at the back where I know there's an open fire. There will probably be people sitting there, but I have to help this poor woman because she's shivering so hard I can hear her teeth chattering. As luck would have it, when we get there, two women get up and leave their seats at the fireside, so I gesture at the empty chairs and the woman nods gratefully.

'Can I get you a drink?' I ask and she smiles shyly.

'That would be nice, thank you.' Is that a New York twang lacing her accent?

'What's your poison?'

She frowns, then realises what I meant and nods. 'I'll have what you're having, please.' She sounds like she could have originally come from the West Country and yet there's something of the USA in there too. It's intriguing and I want to find out more.

'Great.'

At the bar, I order two martinis then take them back to the fireside where the woman is removing her coat and hat. When she turns to me, I see her hairline is damp which makes the hair there appear darker than the rest. Her smile lights up her beautiful face and now that her nose is no longer red, I can admire her porcelain skin and the faint roses in her cheeks.

'Here you go.' I hand her the drink and she takes a sip. Her eyes widen and she gives a small cough.

'That's strong.'

'The best way.' I smile as I take one of the chairs and she takes the other. They are side by side, but both tilted slightly to face the fire so I can look at her profile without being too obvious about it. Staring at her would probably make her grab her things and run.

'Thank you so much for this,' she says after a few more sips of the martini. 'I was frozen when I came into the bar and I'm so tired after a long flight. My brain doesn't seem to be computing properly.'

'Where did you fly from?'

She turns to face me now so her body is at an angle on the chair, and she sets the martini glass on her lap while holding it with both hands. 'New York.'

'Wow! One big city to another. Are you here for long?' My voice rises slightly and I cough to clear my throat because I don't want to sound desperate, even though I'm already hoping she is staying for a few nights at least.

She's frowning at me and it makes heat rise to my face. What have I done? Got an olive stuck up my nose? Missed a spot when I trimmed my beard? Or ... have we spent time together before? Come to think of it, she seems vaguely familiar. The problem with sleeping around is that I don't remember every single woman I've fucked and I guess this was bound to happen at some point.

'I'm back in the country for good,' she says. 'I lived in New York for a decade, but I've come home now.'

'So England is home?'

She inclines her head. 'It's strange being back after so long. England was home when I was a child and New York no longer felt like home because ... uhm ... for a while so, yes, I guess England *is* home.'

I can't help wondering what she was going to say about why New York no longer felt like home, but I don't want to press her. Everyone has their secrets and this woman will be no different.

Realising that we haven't exchanged names yet, I say, 'Do I know you? I can't help feeling that we've met before and yet, if you've been in America for ten years then …' I trail off, allowing her the opportunity to take over.

'I feel the same. You look familiar and …' She bites her bottom lip with small, straight white teeth, and my cock jumps to attention. *Fuck, she's hot.* She has that innocent thing going on and yet within her eyes there's the suggestion of more, of something wild and primal, even if it's as yet untapped. I'd like to tap it, that's for sure. 'What's your name?'

'Lucas.' I watch as her eyes widen.

'Lucas Barrett?'

'The one and only.' God, I'm an arrogant prick sometimes.

'I thought I knew you. I'm Carla. Carla Russell.'

Somewhere in my memory, the name rings a bell and I try to put the pieces together.

Russell. Carla.

'Sorry, you'd have known me as Carla Williams.'

'Not Dane's little sister?'

Of course. The red hair. Grey eyes. The air of delicious innocence. And yet, the Carla I knew all those years ago was just a little girl. She was straight up and down, had only just started to get some curves when she was about, what, sixteen? But this goddess before me now has curves that could make a grown man weep. Curves that fill out the black wrap top she's wearing beneath her thick cardigan so the top gapes open, exposing a cleavage I could easily bury my cock in. And I have a rather large cock, so that tells you something about her impressive cleavage. Just the thought makes me harden and I shift on the chair.

'That's me.' She looks down at her drink then back up at me and I note it as a flirtatious gesture, wondering where this could go tonight.

'When did you get all grown up?'

'I'm almost thirty, Lucas.'

Of course, she was almost seven years younger than us. To be honest, I took little notice of her back then, but why would I? I was looking for a good time and she was just a child. Pretty, with her pale skin and freckles, but still too young to do what I was interested in doing.

'So you're back from the Big Apple? How come?' I can't help asking now because I want to know why she's alone and wearing what I assume is a wedding ring.

'Oh ... It's complicated.' She purses her lips then exhales through them. 'It was just time to come back.'

'I'm glad.'

My comment makes her meet my eyes again and I see a flash of something in her grey gaze that makes me even more curious. What happened to this beautiful woman? Did someone hurt her? Or did she hurt them?

'How's your brother?' I realise I should ask. 'I haven't seen him in a while.'

Wynter Wilde

'He lives in Australia now.'

'Of course he does! Actually, I think I saw him a few years back ... probably about eight years ago ... when he was visiting some friends in the UK. Over the years, we lost touch. Of course, life is busy, and people drift apart, but I'd like to catch up with him sometime.'

'Have you been busy with work and your family?' Her eyes flicker to my left hand.

'With work, definitely. I work for a large construction company and it's very busy. But not with family, no. I'm single.' As I say this, I hold her gaze so she can understand that I'm free for some fun if she's up for it, too.

'You're in construction? I never had you pegged as a builder.'

This makes me laugh. 'No, I'm part of the management team, and a shareholder, of a company that oversees construction projects. I don't actually do any building myself.'

'I see. Management, eh?' She glances at the Rolex on my left wrist. 'And you're doing well? I wasn't sure if that was real.'

Laughing, I nod. 'Yes, it's real. And yes, I'm doing all right, I guess.' Well this is a fun game. For once, I'm speaking to a woman who doesn't know I'm incredibly wealthy, and it's kind of refreshing. She's talking to me for reasons other than my bank balance and that's nice. Usually, it's my money or rumours of the baseball bat between my legs that get women interested. And my incredible charm does the rest, because I do know how to charm the ladies.

'I'm glad things have worked out for you,' she says.

'What about you?'

'What about me?'

'What do you do for a living?'

'Oh ... I uhhh... I'm between jobs.'

'Really?' This interests me. 'What were you doing in New York?'

She takes a sip of her drink. 'I worked for a children's charity in the HR department and ... as a hotel cleaner.'

'A cleaner?' I feel my brows knitting above my nose. 'Why the two jobs?'

Her cheeks flush and she blinks. 'Life is expensive and my job with the charity didn't pay very well. I needed to be based in the city so I didn't have a long commute as some days I had a very early start and often worked late into the evenings. Also, it was part of the dream I had to live there for a while, but with health insurance and rent and everything else, one salary didn't cover it.'

'Are you transferring to a branch of the charity here? Or perhaps of the hotel?'

She shakes her head. 'I figured it's time for a change and to be honest, if I can avoid cleaning any more hotel bathrooms, I'll be over the moon.'

'Look at the snow!' someone from the bar shouts and there's a chorus of gasps. I get up and peer across the bar to the windows overlooking the street. Sure enough, it's thumping down.

Turning back to Carla, I see her down her drink, then open her bag. She pulls out a smartphone, rubs the screen, then drops it back in the bag.

'Everything all right?' I ask.

'My stupid old phone died in the taxi from the airport, and I've mislaid the charger.'

'Where are you staying? I'm guessing you didn't intend to head back to Devon tonight?'

'I was going to stay in London for a few days and try to soak up the festive atmosphere.'

'So you've booked a hotel?'

She places her glass on the table to the side of her chair, then shakes her head. Her eyes fill with tears, and she rubs at them. 'I … I tried, but everywhere was booked unless I travel further out and I …' Her bottom lip wobbles. 'I have little money. And now it's snowing heavily and I … I …' Tears rush down her cheeks and something in my chest squeezes.

'Hey, don't cry.' I reach for her hands and take them in mine, meet her gaze, those grey eyes filled with anguish now looking more like storm clouds than pearls. 'I have a big apartment not far from here and you're welcome to stay with me tonight.'

'W-with you?' she asks.

'Why not? I have plenty of room. You need a place to stay and it's not like we're strangers, is it? I grew up with your brother, after all, and I knew you when you had braces and a mass of ginger frizz.' *Shit! Why did I say that?* 'Not frizz ... your hair was always wavy, I meant.'

She's smiling at me through her tears and I find my hand takes on a life of its own and reaches up and strokes her tears away. Her pupils dilate, shiny black circles that reflect my face. Then I remember the wedding ring and I lower my hand. She's married, *and* she's the little sister of my childhood best friend. Nothing can happen here, but I will take her home and offer her a bed for the night. That's what any decent human being would do for an old friend. And I am a decent human being, whatever some of my former conquests might say about me. I never leave a lady unsatisfied and I would never expect one to sleep on the streets.

'Come on then,' I say, standing and shrugging into my coat, then helping Carla with hers. 'Let's get going before it gets any worse.'

I grab the handle of her suitcase and lead the way through the bar, my heart sinking when I see exactly how heavy the snow is now. It's going to be a chilly walk home.

'Here,' I say, offering my left arm to Carla. 'You might want to hold on because it'll be slippery out.'

She slides her arm through mine and holds on tight as we step out into the blizzard. She feels so petite and feminine at my side and something primal rises inside me. The urge to get this woman home safe and sound. To protect her from harm. And to find out if she wants to sleep alone or if she'd like me to warm her bed.

Chapter 5
Carla

We trudge through the snow and I keep my head down, letting Lucas lead me. This all feels so surreal, but then after the nightmare that my life has been for the past ten months, nothing shocks me now. What are the chances of bumping into my brother's childhood best friend in London on a night like this? Probably smaller than I think, but hey, I'm not looking a gift horse in the mouth, I'm just relieved that I have somewhere to stay. I didn't know what I was going to do, but somehow, this man has become my knight in shining armour and he's offered me a bed for the night. Perhaps someone is looking down on me from heaven and keeping me safe after all.

When Lucas stops walking, I have completely lost all sense of direction. I have no idea where we are, but when he leads me through a door manned by a security guard, I am reassured. Even if Lucas has by some chance turned into a murdering psychopath, at least the security guard will be a witness to my final whereabouts.

Starting Over With the Billionaire

The entrance hallway to the building is warm, and it's such a relief to be out of the snow that I feel my body sag. Lucas crosses to a lift and I follow, taking care not to slip on the tiled floor. We enter the lift and I try not to look at the bedraggled mess staring back at me from the mirrored walls. I look like a drowned rat that's been dragged through a hedge backwards. Lucas must think the years have not been kind to me at all.

The lift shoots upwards and soon, the doors open straight into an apartment.

'You have the penthouse?' I ask as we walk inside. Lamps create a golden warmth in the corners of an open plan space and I can see from the doorway that the windows are floor to ceiling. From here, snow flies past the glass, creating the sense that we're inside a cloud. It's a strange sensation and one that makes me feel somehow cosy and yet slightly claustrophobic. We must be really high up and it makes me wonder what the view is like on a fine day.

'I do,' Lucas says, answering my question as he parks my suitcase, then removes his coat and hangs it on the stand near the door. I peel my wet coat off and it's a relief to get the weight of it off my shoulders. My hat follows and I gather my hair over my right shoulder and attempt to tame it, but I know it's going to turn into an unruly mess because it's been soaked and windswept. 'Right, first things first and all that, we need a hot shower and some dry clothes. I meant separate shower, of course.' He smiles but before he looks away, I catch something in his eyes that makes my belly flip.

'That sounds so good.'

Wynter Wilde

'I'll show you to one of the guest rooms and you can get yourself sorted,' he says.

As I follow him through the apartment, I feel a mixture of relief that he meant we'll shower separately and a hint of disappointment. It's been an age since I showered with a man and Lucas is gorgeous. He's grown into a silver fox of a man with his salt and pepper hair and the matching stubble that covers his jaw. He's big and muscular and he smells divine, like lemon grass and ginger and a distinctly masculine scent that is stirring parts of me I thought died months ago. He's the type of man you see on cologne adverts, walking through buildings and speaking directly into the camera with a wicked glint in his eye. He's the type of man women think about when they masturbate while knowing he's unattainable and probably only dates supermodels, reality TV stars or actual foreign princesses.

And I'm going to spend the night at his home.

But we're showering separately, as much as my wanton body seems to be telling me it would like to join him under the hot spray. I don't understand why this is happening to me but I'm tired, I've been shutdown for a long time and I'm doing something I'd never normally do. I guess the best thing I can do now is go with the flow and relax. After all, what have I got to lose? At least I have a bed for the night and I'm out of that dismal December weather. Hopefully, I'll be able to charge my phone and look at getting a train back to Exeter in the morning. I would have liked to stay in London for a few days, but I hadn't banked on snow and the hotels being booked up, so I need to make a sensible decision and try to get my life back on track. How I'm ever going to do that I don't know, but being back in Exeter will help and I'll be able to start over again. Even if starting over was never something I saw in my future because I'd landed the life I wanted and I never imagined letting it go. Sometimes we have no choice, though; that's the nature of things. Our hopes and dreams can come crashing down around us and leave us feeling confused and terrified, lost and directionless.

It's time to slow down, to take stock and to decide what I'm going to do with the time I have left on this planet.

But first, a hot shower, and some dry clothes are in order. Being human means that our basic needs have to be met for our brains to work properly, and the way my jeans are clinging to my legs, cold, damp and heavy, I'm desperate to get them off. I'm also, for the first time in ages, aware that my stomach feels empty and I could use a decent meal. Perhaps Lucas has something here we can eat because I'm going to struggle to sleep with my stomach rumbling like this.

'Shower then food,' Lucas says as if reading my mind, as he shows me into one of his guest rooms and I could weep with gratitude. 'See you in twenty minutes.'

He smiles as he closes the bedroom door behind him, and I'm left alone to admire my surroundings, which are pretty impressive indeed.

Chapter 6

Lucas

After I've showered, I head to the kitchen and set about making some dinner. I'm not a bad chef and can put my hand to pretty much anything, but when it's just me and I'm late home from work or my ... extra-curricular activities, I tend to grab something easy or eat out. However, if I have guests over, I do make an effort. This evening, I have a guest and so I intend on creating a tasty and nutritious meal.

Now and then, my thoughts stray to the guest room and the ensuite where Carla is in the shower. I can hear the spray running and I can't help imagining what she might look like with her long red hair plastered to her skin, soap suds over her voluptuous body and ... I'm rock hard already and I take a few deep breaths to steady myself. Man, this chick is something else and knowing that she's in my home, in my guest room, is arousing me more than it should. Especially because Carla is not a stranger, and I knew her brother very well growing up. In fact, we were best friends for years and I spent a lot of time at their home. Carla was a cute kid, but to me she was always *my friend's younger sister*, sometimes annoying, sometimes aloof, but always younger and therefore, back then, of little consequence. Am I finding her even more attractive because I know her and her family? Is she forbidden fruit, and that makes me crave her? I don't think there's any reason we couldn't hook up at least once while she's staying here. It's not like she's a child anymore, is it? She's a gorgeous grown woman with a mind of her own. But there is that wedding ring on the third finger of her left hand ... I'm not sure where I stand with that.

Now ... what can we have to drink with our food?

Browsing the wine rack, I select a Rioja that will pair well with it, then decide it will be nice to eat at the table. When alone, I eat at the kitchen island, but with company, I prefer the fancy black table the interior designer told me would look perfect in my luxurious bachelor pad.

Chapter 7
Carla

The shower is incredible and I stand under the spray for far longer than I need to because I don't want to get out. The hot water massages my scalp, caresses my skin and makes me feel clean all over, as well as very relaxed. It's as I'm standing there that I realise exactly how tired I am. In fact, I am positively bone weary and I know it's from months of broken sleep, money worries, and the pain of grief. There is nothing worse than waking every day knowing that you will not see the person you thought you'd spend your life with. When we married, we were so full of joy and hope, and I really thought we'd have years of married life ahead of us. I never suspected for a moment that our time together would be cut short. I envisaged us growing old together, strolling hand in hand around Central Park while our grandchildren skipped ahead. But one night took it all from me and now I'll never have the things I wanted most of all.

I am also, I realise, tired of being *The Widow*. Everyone we knew looked at me with pity in their eyes and that in itself can be wearing. We used to have invites to friends' homes for dinner and celebrations, but since I lost Kofi, the invites dwindled away to nothing. It was like people were worried that their celebrations and happiness would be too much for me and they didn't know how to cope with that, so they decided it would be easier not to include me than to witness my pain. Some still tried, and I was grateful to them, but if I was being honest with myself, it was hard to see their lives going to plan while mine was at a standstill. Their lives went on: their jobs, their home lives, their families grew, while I was alone, single, broken by loss.

But life goes on and I know this well. It's not like we didn't discuss these things during our marriage. The topics no loving couple wants to discuss but knows they must because there are certain things that need to be put in order. Just in case one day your life changes in an instant and is never the same. Just in case you're going to end up alone because your person, your reason for existing, has gone.

Fuck, the pain is harsh and the sense of loneliness and isolation is enough to drive me insane. I have had many days where my grip on reality has felt like it's slipping away and I worry I will soon lose my mind completely. And then I've wondered if that might not be kinder, because if I'm no longer lucid, then I won't feel all these things or need to worry about enduring my loss.

Turning off the shower, I reach for the towel and wrap it around my body, then step out of the spacious cubicle and onto the mat. After wrapping another towel around my hair, I pad through to the bedroom and sit on the edge of the bed.

This evening I have two choices. I can be the widow and see the pity in Lucas' eyes, or I can be me, try to find the woman

I used to be before I fell in love and got married, try to rediscover the me who's still there beneath all the layers that have formed over the past decade. She's still there. I know she is, and that thought gives me hope.

There is a chance that I could have Lucas look at me as a woman and not a widow. I could take this for myself tonight. Kofi always told me he'd want me to find someone else if anything happened to him and I'd swear blind that I wouldn't. But when the scenario was in reverse, I hated the thought of him being alone if anything happened to me, so I guess he was right. It's hard, though, thinking of moving on when you still love someone. But I will always love Kofi. Always. He'll live on in my heart, frozen in time, my wonderful husband, partner and best friend.

For tonight, for the time being, I'll keep my loss to myself. It's not like anything is going to happen. I can remember now what an arrogant prick Lucas could be at times when he was younger, and I thought I saw some of that arrogance still there today. He wasn't always an idiot, but he could be if he was in a bad mood. It could have been because he was a hormonal teen, of course, but I didn't understand all that stuff back then. Tonight, I'm going to allow myself to relax and have some fun. Well, maybe not fun, but at least to relax and be like the Carla I used to be.

Once I've dried, slathered my skin in almond body butter and rubbed anti-frizz serum through my long hair, I apply a rich moisturiser to my face then a slick of gloss to my lips. Nothing about me screams sophisticated socialite and I'm sure that's the kind of woman Lucas is used to, but right now, I don't care. We're here together, literally snowed in, and there's no competition. Just me and an old friend spending the night at his apartment. If the delicious aromas that greet me as I open the door are anything to go by, we are about to enjoy a tasty dinner, too.

The apartment is open plan and I walk from the hallway of bedroom doors to the lounge and then through to the kitchen area. Beyond that is a dining area and I see Lucas has set the table and there's even a candle burning between the place settings. The apartment screams bachelor pad from the dark furniture to the dark grey walls and the hardwood flooring. The thought hits me he's probably fucked women on that hard floor and instead of repulsing me; I find it turns me on. In the lounge area, an enormous TV screen is fixed to the wall and before that is an L shaped black leather sofa that looks comfortable enough to sleep on.

The apartment is clean from the lines of the furniture to the fact that nothing is out of place. Either Lucas is very tidy or he has a cleaner because there's not so much as a book or photograph in sight and not a crumb or stray hair to be seen anywhere. It is a stark contrast to my apartment in New York where the rugs were worn and stained, the sofa springs were sticking out on one side and two of the window frames had warped so the sash windows wouldn't close all the way. The tap in the kitchen also leaked and the upstairs neighbours held loud parties on Saturday nights. But it was home, and it was lived in and Kofi and I felt comfortable there. Something about how tidy Lucas' apartment is makes nerves stir in my belly because why is he so neat and tidy? Does he have OCD or something and he'll freak out if I leave so much as a hair from my head on the floor? Is he a serial killer who keeps everything meticulously clean so he can murder at will? Am I letting my imagination run away with me and worrying about nothing? I groan inwardly because exhaustion is making my brain race and I know I need sleep and soon.

I jump as Lucas appears in the kitchen area from behind the island. He must have been getting something out of a cupboard.

'Feeling better?' he asks.

'Much, thank you. That shower is amazing.'

'The water pressure is great in this building. You were in there so long I thought perhaps you'd been washed down the plughole,' he jokes and I smile.

'I could have stayed in there another twenty minutes easily.'

'Twenty minutes, eh? There's a lot you can do in twenty minutes.' There's a twinkle in his eye and it does something to my insides. Is he being wicked or am I reading into things? 'Like whip up a tasty meal for a guest. Have a seat at the table.'

'Don't you want a hand with anything?' I ask, then bite the inside of my cheek. God, if we're talking in innuendos, that could have sounded rather blatant. 'I mean ... Can I help with anything?'

'It's all under control,' he says.

Lucas comes out from behind the island and pulls out a chair at the table so I sit down. He smells so good, the scent I encountered earlier but now fresh and tantalising. He's wearing dark grey lounge pants and a navy T-shirt, and I can't help noticing the way the top hugs his broad shoulders, and as he returns to the kitchen area, the way the trousers accentuate firm, rounded buttocks ripe for squeezing.

Closing my eyes at the image, I swallow hard. This isn't me. I don't ogle men. I've been faithful for so long. Perhaps parts of me are waking after a long slumber and this is part of the healing process. Who knows? It's nice to feel again and yet it saddens me because I don't want to let go of my life in New York. I don't want to let go of Kofi and yet I know I have to if I'm to have any sort of life going forwards.

'Wine?' Lucas asks.

'Yes, please.'

He brings a bottle of red and two large glasses to the table, then pours with the finesse of a sommelier. 'Here.' He hands me a glass and I raise it to my nose, inhale aromas of balsamic, liquorice, red fruits, and spice. When I take a sip, it's smooth but complex and I can taste dark fruits, tobacco, oak, and vanilla.

'This is delicious.' Looking up I find Lucas watching me, something in his eyes that makes my stomach flip over. He licks his lips and for a moment I think he will lean over and flick his tongue over my lips to taste the wine there. If he did, what would I do?

'It's a Bodegas Ollauri Rioja Tinto. 2004. Not costly, but delicious. I'm glad you like it.'

'I do like wine, especially red wine.' What I don't add is that I couldn't afford to drink it very often because money was so tight.

'Well, enjoy it because there's plenty more where that one came from.' He gestures across the room and I see the floor to ceiling wine rack full of wine bottles. He really is loaded. 'Dinner won't be long.'

'It smells incredible. What are we having?'

'Wild mushroom risotto. If I'd known I was having company, I'd have made something a bit more adventurous, but this is quick and very tasty.'

'It sounds amazing.'

He brings a long plate of garlic bread topped with freshly cut herbs to the table along with a bowl of black and green olives that glisten with oil.

'Help yourself,' he says.

There are small olive forks set in the sides of the bowl, so I take one and spear an olive then raise it to my lips. The salty flavour and slick oil coat my tongue and I close my eyes for a moment to savour them. When I open my eyes, I reach for my wine and enjoy the rich flavour and the silky texture. It hits me that I'm experiencing sensations I haven't felt in what feels like a lifetime. This man is tempting my senses with food and wine and with a power shower that could have made me come had I allowed it to hit the right angle at the apex of my thighs. It's a heady combination and my shoulders drop, my breath emerges in a gentle stream and I begin to unwind. This is what I've needed but not known how to access. Another human being is taking care of me, and it feels good.

When Lucas brings plates of green salad to the table, followed by steaming bowls of risotto and a small bowl of grated parmesan, my mouth waters. The rice looks creamy and the mushrooms are cooked to perfection and he has sprinkled freshly chopped parsley over the top. I lift my fork, keen to tuck in.

'Cheers, Carla.' He raises his glass and I put the fork down, embarrassed that I was so eager to eat, and pick up my glass.

'Cheers, Lucas. And thank you. For this room, the shower and for this food. I'm so grateful and I don't know what I could possibly do to thank you.'

He meets my eyes over the table, and his pupils dilate. The corner of his mouth lifts slightly and I see something flicker across his face that puzzles me. It's mischievous. Wicked. Lustful?

'I'm sure we can think of something if we put our heads together later,' he says, and my breath catches in my throat.

What. The. Fuck?

I don't understand him and yet my nipples harden to peaks under my silky soft bamboo long sleeved top. I'm not wearing a bra because I couldn't be bothered to dig one out of my case, but I thought it would be OK because it's warm in the apartment. Now though, I could stab a mushroom with the hard peaks beneath my clothing and I see Lucas' eyes flicker downwards for a fraction of a second and know that he's seen what's going on under my top. Being aware that he's witnessed this does something to me lower down, and I squeeze my thighs together under the table, aware of a tingling down there that has nothing to do with food and wine. It's all about this man who's looking at me like it's me he wants to eat and not the food on the table.

For a moment, I picture him sweeping the food aside and reaching for me, pulling me onto the table top then stripping away my clothes. I'd be naked in front of him and he'd want me. He'd push my thighs open and kiss the soft flesh there, run his fingers over my hips and then down. His lips and fingers would meet in the middle and press hot possessive kisses to my—

'Parmesan?' Lucas is frowning at me. 'Carla? Are you all right?'

I shake myself inwardly, then nod. 'Yes.' My voice is a squeak. I cough. 'Yes. Sorry. I think it's jetlag setting in. Parmesan would be great.'

Bloody liar!

My cheeks blaze and I take a gulp of wine.

So now I'm having fantasies about being eaten out on the table of a childhood friend. Imagining what those full lips would feel like as they devoured me, suckled me, ate me like a three-course meal.

Oh fuck...

Lucas Barrett must be the devil in disguise because I've only been inside his home for a short time, and he's already got me thinking about getting hot and heavy with him. This isn't me. I'm not like this.

Or am I and I've simply forgotten as life has taken over and dragged me down?

I still love my husband. But I also know he's gone.

Could Lucas be the key to rediscovering the old me?

'Well tuck in because your blood sugar is probably low,' he says, waving his fork at my plate.

'Yes. I think it is.' Of course that's what it is, along with jetlag and grief.

I raise a fork of risotto to my mouth and as soon as I taste it; I moan. It's delicious and I'm suddenly ravenous.

But as I fill my belly, I realise that it's not just risotto I'm ravenous for ...

Chapter 8

Lucas

Watching Carla eat is a deeply sensual experience, and my cock presses against the thick fabric of my lounge pants throughout the meal. I find it hard to concentrate on my food because of how Carla's full breasts wobble under her top as she moves and how her hard nipples strain against the fabric, tempting me. Are they pale pink or dark? Is the areole wide or small? Will they fill my mouth when I suck them?

Wait, *when?*

I want to know more than I should.

'The snow is getting worse,' I say in an attempt to distract myself. If my erection doesn't go down, I won't be able to get up from the table. The thought of standing and whipping it out then asking her to take me in her mouth occurs to me, but that's just the devil inside me and not something I'd ever do. Well ... not to Carla perhaps, but it has been done before. I'm a man with a raging libido, for fuck's sake. What's wrong with that? The majority of women I've been with like being told what to do in the bedroom. Of course, I like it when they take charge too, but only within limits. There's something inside me that likes to dominate and so I don't fight it.

Carla looks up from her food and across to the windows. The snow is coming down hard and I know she's probably feeling like we're trapped inside a cloud. I get that here when it rains and snows and I kind of like the sense of being isolated. This evening, it's like Carla and I are the only people left in the world and we have the rest of time stretching out ahead of us.

Whatever will we do to keep busy?

'More wine?' I ask, but I fill her glass without waiting for a reply. The smile she rewards me with tells me that Carla probably likes a man who takes charge, too.

'Thank you.' She takes a sip without breaking eye contact and if it's possible, my cock grows even harder.

If this is the main course with Carla, then I can't wait for dessert.

Chapter 9

Carla

'That was the best meal I've had in years,' I say as I help Lucas clear the table.

'Seriously?' He raises his brows.

'Seriously. You're an amazing cock.' *What the very fuck?* 'Oh my god, I meant cook! You're an amazing cook!'

He's grinning at my error but he shrugs and gives a deep laugh. 'Why thank you, my lady. I'm glad you enjoyed it.'

'Do you *cook* like that often?' *Why did I say cock?* Yes, I was having some inappropriate thoughts as we ate, and yes, I could see the outline of what looks like a very large cock in his lounge pants, but did I have to say cock? Placing the plates on the side, I go back for the garlic bread dish.

'Not every night. There doesn't seem much point when it's just me.' He opens a concealed dishwasher and starts loading it. 'Doesn't your husband cook for you?'

I freeze like I've been shot and tighten my grip on the dish.

What do I say now? I don't want to tell Lucas the truth and yet I don't want to lie.

'No.' My answer is short and sharp. 'Not anymore.'

'Oh...' Lucas grimaces, then accepts the dish that I hold out and places it in the top rack of the dishwasher. 'Sorry about that.'

'Shall I get the glasses?' I look over at the table, knowing that I probably shouldn't drink more wine, but I have a thirst rising inside me and I don't feel like water will quench it.

'I could open another bottle,' he says, and I almost sag with relief.

'That would be lovely.'

He adds a tablet to the dishwasher, then closes it. 'I'm sorry, Carla.'

'Whatever for?'

'For mentioning your husband. It's clearly a difficult topic for you and I don't want to make you uncomfortable. I just assumed because you're still wearing the ring that ... well ... you were still together.'

My eyes drop to my left hand and I touch the inside of the gold band with my thumb. 'It's hard to take it off. I'm kind of used to wearing it.' That's not a lie because it is hard to think about removing it. That would be like accepting that Kofi is gone forever.

'And I guess wearing it means that you don't get creeps hitting on you all the time, right?' Lucas laughs, but I have to suck in a breath. There are many reasons I still wear the ring, but I can't share them with him right now. This evening I am not Carla the widow, but Carla the woman. The single woman.

'I don't mean to sound rude but could we talk about something else?' I ask. 'Please?'

'Of course. No problem at all. Tell me how your brother's getting on.'

So I do, while he opens more wine and I grab the glasses and we take them through to the lounge area and sit at opposite ends of the sofa.

'Hold on for two minutes.' He gets up and jumps over the back of the sofa in a way that shows agility but also a kind of youthful side of him. When he returns, he holds out a black bowl and a spoon. 'For you.'

'What is it?'

'Take a look.' His smile is infectious and I smile back then accept the bowl.

'Chocolate ice cream?'

'Your favourite, right?'

'You remembered?' He could just be guessing because the odds are that chocolate could be my favourite flavour, but he's not wrong.

'I did. This is from a deli not far from here and it's the best I've ever tasted.'

I try it, and it really is delicious. 'OMG.'

'I know!' He fetches his own bowl, then we sit on the sofa while he flicks through the channels. 'See anything you fancy?'

'I haven't seen that new Tom Cruise movie or the Benedict Cumberbatch one.'

'Do you have a preference?'

'Not really.'

'OK then ... We'll go with the latter.'

The movie starts and I polish off my ice cream, then sip my wine. I am warm and full and blissfully relaxed. The seats of the sofa are deep, and I feel like I'm being cushioned on air. The leather is warm and smooth and before I know it, I'm struggling to keep my eyes open.

'Put your feet on me if you like.' Lucas reaches for them and rests them on his lap as if we do this every day, then pulls off my fluffy socks and massages my feet. My body weakens, my eyes close, and I allow myself to drift along on a cloud of sensation.

His hands are strong as they work my feet, easing out tension and making my body melt. The sofa cushions me like a giant hug and the TV fills the room with dialogue and occasional music. Outside, the wind howls, and the snow is whipped past the windows, but inside we are cocooned in a cosy space.

Just the two of us.

Lucas Barrett, billionaire businessman.

And me. Carla Russell. Daughter. Sister. Widow. Woman. Person of no fixed abode and no career to speak of, but with a heart filled with love for her family and a wobbly sense of hope that the future will be kind.

The Lucas I remember from childhood differed greatly from the Lucas I am getting to know today. I suppose that when he wasn't being grumpy, there was always a kindness to him. Until today, I had forgotten the warmth of his smile and the depth of his laughter, how it could reach down inside me and coax my own mirth. Sometimes memories are buried deep, and those memories might not always be significant ones, but a smell, a song, a glimpse of something can trigger recollections both good and bad. For me, this evening, I am hosting a whole load of memories. Lucas is more than a rich playboy, even if that's the role he's currently enacting. He is so much more. And I feel safe here with him.

The question is whether he wants me to see who he is or whether he maintains the façade because it's what he's got used to over the years. I know only too well what it's like to pretend to be fine, to pretend to be coping when inside I am raw as sunburn and ache like I've been punched all over.

Right now though, I am enjoying being touched. The hands on my feet are not hands of pity or hands of desire, they are the hands of a friend soothing and relaxing me. Simply being touched is delightful after the absence of so much as a gentle caress. It's as if Lucas knows this and so he keeps kneading out the tension and I fall deeper into this trance of ecstasy until I teeter on the edge of sleep.

I finally submit to it, knowing that for tonight at least, I am not alone.

Chapter 10

Lucas

When I wake the next morning, my apartment is filled with a strange hazy light. I pad out to the lounge and see that it's still snowing. Crossing to the windows, I peer out and can just about make out the buildings opposite and the ground below, but the snow keeps flying past and I realise that it's not stopping soon.

The apartment, thankfully, is warm with its underfloor heating and double glazing, so I'm wearing a T-shirt and lounge pants. Unusually for me, I slept past five this morning, then lay in bed for a bit, thinking about last night and how strange it was.

After filling my mug with coffee, I take a sip and savour the robust flavour and the instant surge of caffeine. I take a few more sips, then return to the window and gaze at the white canvas below that appears in flashes between flurries of snow.

About last night ... Nothing happened. Not really. We watched a movie, and I gave Carla a foot massage and it was both pleasant and somewhat erotic — for me at least. Carla was exhausted and so she dropped off to sleep almost as soon as I touched her pretty little feet. We talked a bit over dinner, but she wasn't keen to discuss her husband, or is it ex-husband? I'm not sure and I didn't want to press her for details. I'm not keen on the idea of being the other man, if she is still married, but I also wouldn't want to miss out on getting a feel of those killer curves if that's what she's up for. *Oops!* Just the thought of them makes me hard, and I brush my free hand over the bulge in my trousers, keen for some relief.

'Down, boy,' I say with a laugh. I wonder if Carla likes morning sex ...

Last night, I woke her when the movie finished, and she plodded to bed after thanking me again for the food and wine, as well as the room for the night. And then we went our separate ways. In all honesty, I was tired by then too, so I brushed my teeth, got into bed and dropped off quite quickly. Something about knowing there was another person in the apartment was quite comforting. Weird really, because I enjoy living alone.

But now I'm wide awake and raring to go, so I'll take her a coffee and see how she reacts. Not much else we can do this morning other than fuck anyway because with that blizzard, no one's going anywhere this side of noon.

Coffee made, I knock gently on Carla's door and when I hear her murmur *Hello?* I push the door open.

'Morning.' I place the coffee on the bedside table, then smile down at her. Her red hair is spread out over the pillow and her right arm is hooked over the duvet, but the rest of her is hidden from view. Her skin is milky white against the navy cotton of the pillowcase, and her hair looks darker than it is because the only light is coming from the hallway. It makes me think of a spirit or faerie in a fantasy novel because she's almost too beautiful to be real. And she's here in *my* guest room. 'How did you sleep?'

She frowns then sits up, and the duvet falls away, revealing a fitted white vest top. I avert my eyes because otherwise I'll stare at those incredible breasts.

'Not too bad, I think. Oh ... I fell asleep last night on the sofa, didn't I? I'm so sorry, Lucas, you must think I'm so rude.'

'Not at all. You were exhausted. Do you feel better now?' There's hope in my tone and I sigh inwardly because I don't want to sound desperate.

Carla rubs a hand over her brow, then shakes her head. 'I'm really sorry, but ... I don't feel at all well. Everything's a bit ... spinny.'

'Spinny?' I lean forwards as concern grips me. 'In what way?'

'I feel kind of dizzy and lightheaded.'

'Lie back down then.' I lift the duvet slightly so she can scoot down and she does, her hair fanning out over the pillow again. 'Do you want some water or juice instead of the coffee?'

'Water would be great, thanks.' She peers up at me. 'This is so embarrassing.'

'Don't be silly. You've probably caught a chill from getting soaked and frozen last night and you could have picked something up on the flight, too.'

'I guess so. That's how I feel ... chilled to the bone.'

'Right, I'll get you a lemon and honey too, then you can go back to sleep. If need be, I can call my doctor to come and check on you.'

'Is it still snowing?' she asks.

'Heavily.'

'Oh god ... How am I going to get a train back to Devon?'

The worry on her face tugs at my insides, and I shake my head. 'You're not going anywhere today because of the snow and because you're not feeling well.'

'Lucas, I don't want to put you out.' She tries to sit up again, but then she winces and flops onto the pillow, pressing a palm to her forehead.

'You're not putting me out at all. It's nice to have some company, and it looks like we're going to be snowed in for a few days, so it's the perfect time for you to rest.'

I head to the kitchen and tip her coffee down the sink, then I make a virgin hot toddy and pour some filtered water into a glass and take them back to her. After I've set them on the bedside table, I crouch next to the bed. 'Try to drink that while it's warm.' I point at the lemon and honey.

'I will, thanks.'

She sits up, and I help her by plumping the pillows behind her.

'I must look a state.' She pushes her hair back from her face and gives a small laugh. 'I feel dreadful.'

'I'll get you some painkillers as well.'

'Lucas, thank you. I really am sorry about this. I had every intention of getting out of your hair today and going back to Mum and Dad's in Devon.'

'Are they there?' I ask.

'They're in Australia until the New Year. They're staying with Dane.'

'So if you go back, who'll be with you over the holidays?' This is none of my business, but I can't help asking.

She takes a sip of the lemon and honey, then meets my eyes. 'I'll be alone. But it's fine. I don't mind. I'm kind of used to it.' She bites her bottom lip then, as if she's said too much, and I move to perch on the edge of the bed.

'I'm sure your parents and Dane wouldn't want you to be alone.'

She gives a small shrug. 'It's OK. I could have gone to Australia too, but I wanted to get back to the UK and settle in.'

'You're not going back to New York?'

'No. Not for a while, anyway.'

'Well, look ... you're not feeling well and you've no one at your parents' home to rush back to, so why don't you give yourself a break and stay here for a few days? There's no point in you rushing back and you know ... I could show you around London once the snow slows down. We could do some touristy things if you like?' *Who even am I this morning?* It must be because I know Carla from way back when, because this is so not me.

'I can't ask that of you, Lucas. And don't you have work?'

'Not today because it's Saturday and we can work around my job, anyway. That can all be sorted. But first, you need to get well and the best way to do that is to rest.'

'I don't know how to thank you.'

'Carla ...' I reach out as if to brush her hair from her cheek, then think better of it and lower my hand. 'I'm sorry you're not feeling well, but I can't pretend it's not good to see you again. There's a lot from our childhoods that I've forgotten, but I remember having some good times at your home.'

'Dane thought a lot of you, as did my parents.'

'I thought a lot of them, too. I was round their house a lot in my teens.' *Is that a pang of nostalgia?* I'm not usually one to indulge in sentimentality. Perhaps it's my age because I am on the fast train to forty.

'I remember,' she says with a smile.

She holds my gaze then and I see things in her eyes that I don't fully understand and yet they tug at my heart. There are memories buried deeply inside both of us that go back a long way. I know memories are subjective and we might both recall things differently, but the feeling I'm getting here from Carla is that there was a fondness between us. Hers for me and ... yes, mine for her, even if it wasn't necessarily sexual back then. If I had a sister and she was in

Australia alone and needed a place to stay, I'd want Dane to help her. Not to fuck her, no, but to be there for her, yes.

'Let me get those painkillers for you, then you can sleep some more.' Before I know what I'm doing, I raise her hand and press a kiss to the palm. She smells of vanilla and pomegranate and something else, a distinctly female scent that stirs my loins. My mouth waters and my cock twitches then I chastise myself because she's not well. Rule number one is *Don't get horny with a sick person.*

I gently release her hand, then get up and leave the room, hoping she'll stay for a few days so I can take care of her and worship that killer body and she can get well again.

So I can take care of her? And worship that killer body?

Whoa ... That is not what I meant! The red wine must have addled my brain because I'm all out of sorts this morning. I need to do a workout, lift some weights, get sweaty and remind myself who I am. But first I'll get Carla some painkillers and perhaps a cold cloth for her fevered brow.

Chapter 11

Carla

Four days pass with me in the bed in Lucas' guest room. During that time, he is kind and attentive, bringing me drinks, snacks, and painkillers to lower my temperature. If I didn't feel so ill, I would have worried more about the imposition but I sleep a lot. In fact, it's like I haven't slept in years and I am catching up. Lucas tells me that the snow continues outside and that the drifts are building on the pavements and against buildings. Apparently it's the heaviest snow the UK has had in decades. He also tells me he's been out for some groceries twice and I'm amazed that he braved the weather but he shrugs my praise off and says we have to eat.

When I finally feel well enough to leave the bed, Lucas helps me to the lounge and sets me up on the sofa there with pillows and a soft, warm blanket. He hands me the TV remote and places a glass of water on the table in front of me.

'Don't you need to get to work?' I ask.

'I'm working remotely.' He sits on the end of the sofa. 'Edward can't get to the office and neither can a lot of company employees, so we've advised that travel should only be attempted if absolutely necessary. Our employees are all issued with staff laptops and so they can work from home when necessary and those who live outside of Central London often work from home for most of the week.'

'It sounds like an excellent company to work for.' I take a sip of the water, which is cold and refreshing.

'We pride ourselves on being an adaptable and considerate employer. It's the best way to recruit the best of the best.' His grin makes my stomach do a little jump. I can just imagine him at work in a smart business suit, his hair combed back from his broad forehead, his jaw dusted with that sexy salt and pepper stubble and his voice firm and commanding as he issues instructions to his staff. I'm sure he has many admirers swooning with desire every time he walks past their desks. A stab of jealousy pierces my chest and I rub at the spot as if to soothe it away. Whatever do I have to feel jealous about? Lucas is an old friend of my brother and nothing more.

'Is your chest OK?' he asks, his eyes filled with concern.

'Yes.' Nodding, I take another sip of water. 'I'm feeling much better now, thank you.'

'I'm relieved. You had me worried there, especially when I came to check on you and found you delirious. I thought I'd have to carry you out to the limo and get you to A and E. Although, having said that, I'm not sure the limo would have made it through the snow, so we'd have had to get the company Range Rover on the road instead.'

'Thankfully not.' I smile and shift my position on the sofa. 'Lucas ... I'm so grateful to you for looking after me. And for speaking to my parents.'

My mother called my phone the afternoon of my first full day here and I was too poorly to speak to her, so Lucas did instead. Mum was surprised to find out I was staying with Lucas, but he soon reassured her and Dad that I was in safe hands and then he had a brief phone catchup with Dane. I know all this because he told me and then Mum sent me a message that evening to let me know she thought Lucas was very charming and was happy to know he was taking care of me. She also said that they didn't mention Kofi because they know I don't like to talk about him to people outside the family. I'm not sure where she got that from, but I didn't argue with her; she does her best and in this case, I'm glad she didn't tell Lucas about him and what happened. Mum worries a lot about me. She was worried about me being alone when I travelled back to the UK but she also said that I'm an adult and as hard as it is for her, she has to accept that I'm old enough to live my life the way I choose. I can understand how hard it must be for her and so I tell her I'm just fine and don't let on when I'm feeling blue or when I'm struggling. She's entitled to her own life and so is Dad and I'm an adult and need to stand on my own two feet, whether or not I'm wobbling on them.

'It was great to speak to them all again. Hopefully, we can meet up in person when they're back in the UK.' Lucas rubs a hand over his hair. 'Are you hungry?'

'Lucas, you've done enough for me.'

'We need to build your strength up.'

'OK then, I am a bit peckish.'

'Give me twenty minutes.'

He gets up and goes to the kitchen and starts pottering around. I lie back and gaze across the room at the windows. The snow seems to have slowed a bit but it's still falling. We had snow like this in New York during the winters and sometimes it would go on for weeks. But out there they seem to cope much better than we do in the UK. It's like here, the extremes of weather cause things to come to a standstill and it takes people a while to get going again. Although Lucas did say that locals have made an effort to dig others out and to keep things running so perhaps it's getting better. All I know for certain right now is that I am lucky I bumped into Lucas and that he was prepared to take care of me. If he hadn't, I have no idea how I would have managed. I'd have been forced to find a hotel room outside of Central London and to pay through the nose for the pleasure probably, either maxing out a credit card or blowing my rainy-day savings. After that, I'd have had to make my way back to Devon to spend Christmas and New Year alone. The latter is still an option obviously, but at least I've been able to stay here with Lucas and not squander money I don't have on a hotel room.

'One bowl of chicken noodle soup for my lady.' Lucas appears at my side, holding a tray.

'Wow! That was fast.' I sit upright, and Lucas carefully places the tray on my lap.

'I made it last night while you were sleeping, so all I had to do was heat it up. Do you want a slice of bread or toast with it?'

'This is great, thanks.'

I eat slowly, savouring the soup that is packed with protein and colourful vegetables. It's delicious and I polish off the bowl. Lucas has a bowl of his own, then he takes our empty bowls out to the kitchen. When he returns he has two mugs of tea and a plate of cookies.

'Don't tell me you made them too,' I say.

'Unfortunately not. But they are delicious. I picked them up from the deli along with some more olives and ciabatta that I got for tonight.'

'You're spoiling me, Lucas.'

'Not really.' He shrugs. 'I enjoy eating too.'

'I was hoping I'd lose a few pounds while I was unwell, but at this rate you'll have me packing it all back on.'

His brows meet and his eyes darken. 'Don't say that, Carla.'

'What do you mean?'

'Don't put yourself down like that. You obviously have no idea how fucking gorgeous you are.'

'You think I'm gorgeous?' Kofi did, I know that, but he was my husband and best friend and we'd been together long enough for me to feel secure. I knew he'd love me if I put weight on or lost it because it was me he loved and not my appearance. Although he enjoyed my curves and told me so often enough. Did I take that for granted too?

'I think you're stunning and I don't even want to hear you putting yourself down again. Not while you're staying under my roof. Is that clear?'

His strict tone takes me by surprise, but it also makes me tingle between my legs. I like this side of him. It's so masculine and it makes me feel feminine and there's something about that which appeals to me on a deeper level.

'Crystal clear,' I say, holding his gaze. I run my tongue over my lower lip, then give it a nibble with my teeth. It's suggestive I know, but I want to see how he reacts.

His pupils dilate and his lips part. He stares at my mouth and moves forwards slightly as if he's going to pounce, but then it's like a cloud lifts from his vision and he sits back.

'You need to rest,' he says. 'I'm going to change your bed so you have clean sheets if you need a nap later.'

'There's no need.' I go to get up. 'I can do that.'

A strong hand lands on my shoulder and pushes me backwards so I'm resting against the pillows again. 'You need to rest, Carla.' He comes closer so his body is hovering above me, his face inches from mine. My breath catches as I think he's going to kiss me. I'm at once surprised and confused because I've been ill and must look awful, and yet he doesn't seem to mind. But then he moves slightly and presses a kiss to my forehead. 'Rest.'

He walks away and I lie there, my chest heaving and my core fluttering. Lucas is an enigma. One minute he's kind and gentle and the next he's firm and taking charge. I like both sides of him but wonder who he really is these days. Worrying can make someone short with another person and perhaps that's what's going on here, or perhaps, worst-case scenario, he's getting fed up with me being here and wants me better so I can leave. I'm not good at reading men and I don't know what he wants or thinks and it's all so tiring. Having been married to a man I knew inside out, who I loved with my whole heart, it's so strange being in such close proximity with another man who is, basically, a stranger now. As much as I think I know him from the past, he's a man now and not the boy I knew back then, so he's bound to have changed. Life will have scarred him in some ways, as it scars us all.

And yet he has been so kind and taken such good care of me.

He asked if I wanted to stay for a while so he could show me the sights and I'd like that. I'd also like to get to know him better because I'm curious about who he is now.

I exhale, then close my eyes and allow sleep to claim me. As Lucas said, rest is paramount and I need it to heal.

When I wake an hour later, Lucas reappears from the direction of the bedrooms and holds out a hand. His hair is wet from showering and I note that he's wearing a clean black T-shirt and lounge pants. 'Come on, then.'

'What do you mean?'

'Your bed is fresh now and I've put out clean pyjamas for you.'

'From where?'

'I took the liberty of getting a few things out of your case while you were ill, but then I thought it might be easier if I unpacked everything for you.'

'Oh ... thanks.'

'It'll be easier for you to see what you have if it's in the drawers and wardrobe. Your toiletries are in the bathroom so you can go ahead and shower. Of course, you're welcome to use the toiletries I put in there too. Whatever you like, it's yours.'

He holds my hand and leads me to the bedroom, and I look around. I can't see the case but the bed now has a black and grey duvet cover and sheet on it along with matching pillowcases.

'That's so kind.' I cross the room to the bed and touch the duvet cover. It's soft and cool and makes me want to slide between the sheets and writhe around naked.

'There were ummm ... a few things in the case that I wasn't sure what to do with, so I put them in the ensuite.' Lucas looks down and I think he's being coy, but when I notice his shoulders shaking, I realise that he's laughing.

'What were they?' I ask.

'Your ... toys?'

'Toys?'

He meets my eyes and I can see now that he's grinning. 'Not sure if that's what you call them, but yeah ...'

Shock hits me and my armpits prickle. I know what he's talking about now. *Shitting hell!*

'Don't be embarrassed, Carla. You're a beautiful woman and you're entitled to pleasure yourself. A woman like you should be pleasured regularly.'

Turning, I dash to the bathroom and there, on the side of the sink, are my two vibrators. In the bathroom spotlights they look so bright and colourful and ... on my god I can't believe he saw them and handled them and knows what I must do with them.

In the mirror, I see him appear behind me. He's so tall and broad that he towers over me. He's handsome and masculine and my knees weaken, so I lock them. I see his eyes move to the sink unit and I look that way, too.

There's my purple rabbit vibrator with its g-spot stimulator and those tantalising ears and my air rose with its incredible suction.

'Interesting selection,' he says. I meet his gaze in the mirror and what I see in his eyes strips away my embarrassment. 'Pleasure is everything, Carla. There is no shame in pleasure.'

He runs a hand over my shoulder and down my arm, strokes it up and down in a way that makes my nipples peak and stirs a delicious fluttering between my legs.

He leans closer and whispers in my ear. 'You deserve to be pleasured.'

My eyelids flutter. He's right; bodies are made for pleasure. It has been so long since I've been touched, been held, been close to another human being and I miss it so much.

'I just want you to know that while you're here, I'm at your disposal. Anything you need, Carla ... anything. All you need to do is ask. Or ... if you prefer... you can beg.'

With that, he presses a kiss to the spot beneath my right ear and then nips the lobe, hard enough to make me gasp, but not hard enough to break the skin. Then he turns to leave and walks through to the bedroom, but I can't allow him to go so I follow him.

Starting Over With the Billionaire

'Wait!' My chest heaves and my vision blurs. 'Please, wait.'

I reach for him and step close, press myself against his hard male body and lean against his chest. When he wraps his arms around me, I have to blink hard because the tears fill my eyes and then overflow. I don't know why I'm crying, but I do know I am overwhelmed by need and loss, by everything life has thrown at me and everything that is yet to come. I want to lose myself in this man and escape for a while.

I raise my head and place my hands on his shoulders, feel the hard muscles beneath my palms. He lowers his head and kisses me softly, runs his full lips over my mouth and then trails kisses down my neck to my shoulder. His hands move rhythmically and rousingly on my back and I melt against him. In this moment, he is everything and I want to be with him.

Lucas takes my face in his hands and presses another kiss to my lips, then he says, 'Tell you what. I'm going to wait in here, just in case you feel faint while you shower. If you need me, you call me. Or, you know, if you have something you want to show me ... I'd like that too.'

'To show you?'

'Use that lovely imagination of yours, Carla. I'll be waiting.'

With that, he pulls his T-shirt over his head, and I'm struck dumb by his masculine beauty. The hard planes of his chest and stomach, the dark hair that dusts his chest and abs. His shoulders are broad and strong and my body yearns to feel him over me, under me, behind me, and everywhere.

I breathe deeply, slowly, and pull my top over my head, then step out of my pyjama bottoms. Now it's his turn to gasp and as I walk into the bathroom, I smile. Lucas makes me feel feminine and powerful, aware of my own beauty, yet in awe of his.

Whatever this is between us, I want to explore it. After everything I've endured, isn't it time for me to have something I want? And right now, I want to be in Lucas Barrett's muscular arms.

Chapter 12

Lucas

Watching as Carla undressed has to be one of my all-time hottest moments. I thought I was going to blow my load in my trunks. She is every bit as hot as I knew she would be. She has killer curves and skin I want to touch, kiss, and lick. Her nipples were dusky pink, the areolae a shade darker. Between her legs, the auburn hair was trimmed neatly, and I was allowed a tantalising glimpse of the perfect triangle that sent blood straight to my cock.

When she turned and went into the ensuite, I caught a glimpse of her perfect behind, the cheeks full and round, just begging to be squeezed or bitten.

Fuck, she's sexy!

I hear the shower spray being turned on and sit still, listening. The spray is interrupted as she steps under it. My heart thunders. Am I really going to do this? Our history makes me hesitate for a moment, but then I remember that she's a grown woman and perfectly capable of choosing who she spends time with. It also seems — from what she's said or rather not said — like her husband was a jerk, so she deserves to feel treasured, at least for a while. I've never had any complaints in the bedroom department, so I'm pretty certain I can show her a good time.

So what's making me pause?

A strange feeling in my gut.

Am I nervous? *Me?* After all the women I've fucked over the years, why would I be nervous?

I stand and adjust my trousers over my erection. There's nothing to be nervous about; this is the most normal thing in the world.

Come on, Lucas ... Go get her!

I stride over to the bathroom doorway and take a deep breath, then step into the ensuite. There, in the large shower cubicle, Carla is soaping that glorious body, her skin wet and slippery and covered with frothy suds.

Lucky damned suds!

I stand and watch. Catching sight of me, she smiles wickedly then rubs foam over her breasts. She lifts them in turn, soaps underneath them, then runs her hands to the tight little peaks her nipples have become. She tugs at her nipples so they point in my direction and it's too much; I have to free my cock.

I walk closer, my erection liberated from my lounge pants, and I stroke the shaft. Carla's eyes lower to my groin and she slides her hands down to her belly, then lower ... lower ...

She soaps there, over the hair, then turns slightly to allow the spray to wash the soap away. When she turns back, she opens her legs and runs her right hand down there while the left plays with her breasts, squeezing at her peaked nipples.

Moving closer, I masturbate myself, feeling the tension grow in my cock. My grip is firm, I know how hard I like it, and when I run my hand right to the end of my length, I rub my thumb over the sensitive tip and lubricate myself with my pre-cum. My balls tighten and I know I'm close.

Suddenly, Carla sits down on the floor of the shower and spreads her legs so I can see the dark pink inner lips of that beautiful little pussy. She slides two fingers from her right hand between them and fucks herself while she circles her clit with the fingers of her left hand.

'I'm close, Lucas. So close.' Her voice is barely more than a whisper, yet it reaches my ears, rushes down to my core and grips my cock like a hot mouth.

'Show me.' Crouching in front of the shower, I squeeze my shaft harder. Faster.

'I-I'm coming, Lucas!' She bucks her hips, her fingers pumping in and out of her pussy, and I come too, squirting my seed over the glass of the cubicle, rubbing my shaft until I'm spent.

I tidy myself up then roll onto my back dramatically and laugh. 'Fuck, Carla, that was hot.'

She crawls out of the shower and sits next to me, close enough that I can smell her arousal, see the glistening pink of her sex. I want to touch her and yet I want to wait. This is unusual for me as I'm normally keen to fuck a woman and send her on her way, but this time, something is different. I want to take my time with Carla and savour every second. Plus, I guess, I don't want it to be over quickly because I want her to stay longer.

'Let's get you dressed so you don't catch another chill, then I'll make us something to eat. You need to keep your strength up,' I say. Something is seeping over me and at first I don't recognise it but then I realise it's shyness. Being so intimate with my former best friend's little sister is not familiar. It's kind of strange and yet also hot. But it's more than that. There's something else at play here and I've yet to understand it.

'Why's that?' Carla smiles in a way that makes me want to flip her onto her knees and take her roughly from behind right here. Right now.

'First, because you've been unwell and you're still recovering. Second, because I have plans for you that you'll need energy for.'

'Food it is then.' She leans forwards and her breasts brush my arm then she kisses my cheek before standing up. As she steps over me and grabs a towel from the heated rail, I'm afforded a delicious view of her sex. I've seen a lot of pussy but hers has to be the hottest.

And then she's gone, leaving me with yet another raging hard-on.

I have a strong feeling that having her as a guest is going to be fun...

Chapter 13
Carla

I can't believe what I just did. It was so unlike me, and I've never done anything so brazen before, but then I've never stayed at the apartment of a hot billionaire or had one take such good care of me. Lucas looked after me so well while I was ill, and it awoke something inside me that I quite like. Granted, it's been a while since I had any kind of an erotic encounter with someone and once I started, I couldn't stop. It excited me knowing he was pleasuring himself while he was watching me and when I saw the size of his erection ... He's certainly well endowed. In fact, it made me wonder how it would possibly fit inside me if we ever ... went all the way. Just the thought of it is arousing me again and even though I've just showered, my thighs are slick with my juices. I couldn't resist stepping over him and giving him a close-up view of my pussy as I left the bathroom. I hope he's still thinking about it. The image of him stroking his erection won't leave me for a while, that's for sure.

But now ... I need to put some clothes on before we eat, even though I feel like sliding into that comfortable bed and calling Lucas to join me.

'Not dressed yet?' he asks, his voice low and filled with what I'm hoping is lust.

Turning, I smile, then place my hands on my hips. 'I don't know what to wear.'

He grins as he steps closer to me, lowers his gaze, and caresses me with it. Although his hands don't touch my flesh, I feel like they do and my nipples turn into hard little peaks again, my sex almost hums with need.

When he raises his hands, it's me who steps forwards as if summoned and he brushes the backs of his fingers over my stomach, making me moan.

'Touch me,' I beg, and he laughs softly.

'You want me to touch you?' he asks, raising his brows.

'Please.'

'Here?' he asks, running his fingers over my collarbones.

'Lower.' I bite my bottom lip in anticipation.

'Here?' His eyes darken as he whispers his fingers over my breasts, circles my nipples then tweaks them, making me gasp.

'Yes.'

'How about lower?' He runs his hands down over my belly, then out to my hips before bringing them together at the apex of my thighs. His thumbs stroke the outside of my pussy and then move together, sliding over my mound. I open my legs, desperate to be touched. He reaches around and grabs my behind, then lifts me against him and carries me to the bed where he sets me down on my back so my legs bend at the knees.

He gazes at me, his eyes hungry, then takes my ankles and places them on his shoulders. I can't take my eyes off his, so when he touches my sex, I raise my hips in surprise. I'm sensitive and it feels so good that I move with his fingers as they stroke, rub and circle my clit.

When he slides a finger into me, I cry out and as he adds another, I whimper. He plunders me with two fingers as he rubs his thumb over my clit.

'Is this what you want?' Leaning over me, he seems huge, dominant, almost dangerous. His left hand rests on the bed next to my face, my legs are still against his shoulders. I am completely at his mercy.

'Yes. Please.'

'Why?'

'It feels so good.'

He speeds up, fucking me, rubbing my clit and holding my gaze. His eyes are so dark now they could swallow me whole, and I can't help moving with him, moaning and panting as he takes me to the edge.

But suddenly, he stops.

'Lucas, please!' I reach for him, but he shakes his head and pulls out of me, grabs my hips and flips me over so I'm on my knees on the bed.

'Look at you. Fucking dripping wet for me. Now ... take this!'

He touches me from behind, caressing my labia that are slick with my juices, then I moan as he enters me with two fingers from behind in a way that rubs at my g-spot.

'Touch your clit while I finger you, Carla.'

I rock back and fore as he fucks me, and it's mere seconds before I come all over my fingers and squirt all over his. We move together until my climax wanes and then I flop exhausted on the bed. Lucas lies next to me and holds up his hand.

'That's a lot.' I look at his glistening fingers and the fluid trickling over his palm and laugh.

He moves his hand to his face and sniffs. 'You smell delicious, Carla,' he says, then he slowly licks his hand clean. 'I can't wait to eat you.'

'I can't wait until you do,' I say with a giggle.

'But first ... I really better had make us some food.'

He gives my behind a gentle smack, then gets up and heads to the bathroom where I hear the tap running.

I do not recall the last time I had two mind blowing orgasms so close together, but I have a feeling this won't be the last time with this gorgeous billionaire.

Chapter 14

Carla

Two days later, I am alone in the apartment. Lucas has gone to the office to catch up with some things. I was sad to see him go following yesterday, another blissful day of lounging around while the big chill continued outside. Inside, we were cocooned in a haze of making out on the sofa, in bed and the shower, touching each other but never going all the way. It's kind of fun, like being a teenager again, and I can feel the anticipation building inside me. Of course, I have wondered why Lucas hasn't just fucked me properly but suspect it's a respect thing left over from our childhood. Or perhaps he likes the chase, enjoys delaying the moment of actual penetration because it's even more exciting that way. A small insecure voice at the back of my mind has whispered that it could be because he doesn't find me that attractive, but nothing in the way he treats me would suggest that. I mean, the man has had his fingers inside me and his hands all over me plenty since our initial shower room scene, and it's hard to believe he could do that and lick my juices off his hands if he didn't fancy me. And so I'm enjoying this for what it is; a small sojourn from reality while I'm here in London. At the very least, I figure that the orgasms will replenish my endorphin supplies and so I'm savouring every one while wondering when he'll place his mouth on me and eat me out the way he promised he will. As for that enormous cock of his, I can't wait to feel it inside me, even if I am a bit nervous about how he'll get it all in. We haven't slept together through the night and I'm fine with that because I need my space as I'm sure Lucas does too. After so long alone in bed, it would be strange sleeping next to someone and part of me worries I might roll over in the night and think my Kofi is there. That would be too cruel, too painful, too much to bear. And not at all fair on Lucas.

I'm still in my pyjamas as I walk through the apartment, admiring Lucas' space. I've been here for seven nights now and I love the flow of the apartment, how seamlessly you can move from one room to the next, and as for the gigantic windows with their incredible view of London ... It's breathtaking when the clouds clear and I could stand at the glass for hours just gazing at the view. Buildings of different ages rise towards the sky, varying heights and colours, some with signs on the side and all with windows that glint in the sunlight. Cars and buses weave between them on roads that from here resemble thin grey ribbons, and in the distance the Thames flows, dark and cold but consistent, a reminder of where we are and the history of this magnificent city. The city that Lucas lives and works in. The city he calls home and where he told me he feels he belongs. Home is where the heart is they say, and when Lucas talks about London, I can see the love he has for the city in his eyes and hear it in his voice. He might have grown up in Exeter, but London is where he will stay. Busy, bustling, vast and exciting. So many people and vehicles and buildings and roads. So many hopes and dreams and lives being lived right here. Right below these windows.

Somewhere out there today, Lucas is at work, wearing that expensive suit he dressed in this morning and that cologne that makes me think of morning rain in a forest, woody, earthy and warmed by his skin. Before he left this morning, he kissed me gently, held my gaze with his beautiful blue eyes and told me to help myself to anything I wanted to eat and drink, and to make myself at home. He also suggested that I could rearrange my unpacked clothing to my liking if I'm going to be staying a while, then added that he'd be happy for me to stay until the new year rolls in, if I'd like that too. And I think I would. I have nowhere else to be and no one else to be with, so why not stay here with this enigma of a man? I hadn't bothered to rearrange my clothes in the wardrobe and drawers, but now Lucas has suggested it, I know it feels right.

Once I've made a coffee using the chrome coffee maker in his kitchen, I carry it to my bedroom and set it on the bedside table. Images of yesterday and the day before that tease me. Lucas behind me as I knelt on the bed, his fingers inside me as I masturbated myself. Lucas suckling at my breasts as I held his cock in both hands and rubbed it over my clit, slid him between the lips of my sex and teased us both. Continuing this until he couldn't take it anymore and spurted over my breasts while fingering me until I came too. There is so much pleasure in our coupling that I am aroused now, and so I look around for my vibrator that Lucas used on me last night before leaving me to sleep. I see it at the bottom of the bed tangled up with a T-shirt of his that he gave me to wear. Reaching for it, I grab the T-shirt too and bury my face in it. Lucas is right there with me as I slip the rose vibrator down my pyjama bottoms and allow the suction to sit over my clit. Cross-legged on the bed, I inhale his scent as the vibrator works its magic and as I come quickly; it is Lucas' face I see — his beautiful, perfect face. The man the boy has become. The man I can't wait to see again when he returns from work.

I clean up then open the built-in wardrobe and stare at the clothes and shoes, none of it seeming suitable for this expensive apartment and Lucas' expensive life, but it's all I have and I can't afford to go out and buy new.

I move folded clothes around on the shelves and reorganise dresses and jumpers on the rail, then tuck shoes and trainers neatly at the bottom of the wardrobe. It takes an hour, although I did stop to have another session with my rose when I couldn't stop thinking about Lucas again. My libido has never been this high and I'm guessing it's some sort of emotional and physical reaction to being alone for so long and lost in grief, then being in the presence of a virtual sex god who wants to pleasure me. I mean, what woman wouldn't get horny from being around Lucas? That salt and pepper hair, that sculpted body, that baseball bat between his legs and those piercing blue eyes that seem to bore right through me. He's made for sex and for fantasising about, and I'm making the most of it while I can.

I step back and peer at the top shelf of the wardrobe, wondering if I can reach up there to put the older things I wear less frequently out of the way, when I spot something. It looks like a shoe box. Would Lucas mind if I move it to his room while I'm here? It could be shoes he's never worn or ones he's forgotten about.

Starting Over With the Billionaire

I look around the room and spot the stool tucked under the dressing table, so I get it then set it in front of the wardrobe and climb up. I reach for the box and grab it then step carefully off the stool and go to the bed, intending on leaving it there, but something inside it shifts and the box tilts. Before I can stop it, the lid falls off and the contents spill over the floor.

It seems it didn't contain shoes after all …

Chapter 15

Lucas

In the space of a week, I have become obsessed. I can't fucking believe it, but Carla has got me by the cock and balls. Fuck's sake! I can't stop thinking about her. She's enchanted me with her pretty face, sexy curves, soft as silk skin and that vulnerability in her eyes that makes me want to stride into her past and kill anyone who fucking hurt her. How it's happened, I don't know, but Carla makes me want to wrap her up in a gentle embrace and protect her from the world while also stripping her naked and fucking her so hard she can't walk straight. Like, what's that about? I never get like this about women and never lose sleep over them, but I'm already waking multiple times a night worrying that I've gone too far with her already and that I should let her go straight to Devon right now and tell her never to look back. After all, I'm not good for her; I'm not good for any woman and that's why I make no promises, never commit to any of the women I fuck. I'm honest from the outset and always let them know where they stand and that way no one gets hurt. It's how things are meant to be, but Carla has come along, into my home and my world, and she's changing the natural order of things and making me feel things I've never felt before. This needs to stop. I know it does, but I can't bear to end it yet.

A throat clearing drags me from my reverie and I look across the conference room table to find Edward staring at me, one eyebrow raised in question. I sit up straight in my chair and adjust my tie.

'Everything all right?' Edward asks and I nod. 'You sure?'

'All good.'

'Your guest still with you?' He shuffles a few papers on the table in front of him, a tactic to make me feel like there's no pressure on me, but I can feel the concern emanating from him in waves.

'She is.' Avoiding his gaze, I look across to the windows and watch the small flakes of snow as they swirl down. The snow had stopped for a bit, but the sky looks like there's plenty more up there waiting to come down.

'You could've worked from home today.' Edward leans back in his chair and steeples his fingers under his chin. We've not long finished a meeting and stayed in the room after everyone else had left to iron out a few things before heading to our individual offices.

'I wanted to come in.' It's not a lie. As tempting as it was to stay with Carla, I needed some space, some time to think and breathe. When I'm near her, all I can think about is how much I want to hold her and it's overwhelming me like an addiction. I'm hoping it will fade after I've actually stuck my dick in her. Something about the actual act of sex usually helps me to detach from a woman, and once that's done, she can head back to Devon and I can carry on with my life. However, as I've told myself multiple times recently, I don't want her going home and being alone over Christmas so at least if she stays until the new year then she can see Christmas in with me and I can make sure she's all right. Her brother was my best friend through childhood, and I know her family and so I feel a sense of responsibility towards her. After all, I spent a lot of time with them when I was a kid and they always looked out for me. Plus, I know she had some trouble with her ex that makes her sad sometimes, so looking out for her over the festive season is the decent thing to do.

It's not because I want to spend more time with her at all.

Who am I trying to convince?

'Well, I'm glad you did because we were able sort the issues with that new retail park contract. On a different note, how're you fixed a week tomorrow?'

I frown, trying to work out the day and date.

'It's a Saturday.' Edward laughs. 'I've had the same problem with forgetting the day because of being snowed in at home. It makes you feel like time loses all meaning.'

'I bet Joe's been enjoying it, though.' His little boy is super cute but very energetic and I bet it was an energy drain trying to keep him entertained.

'He has and so has that bloody greyhound.' Edward's smile shows he's speaking fondly as he thinks of Kismet, the greyhound.

'The dog has been enjoying the snow? I thought they were freezing all the time.'

Shaking his head, Edward says, 'Ava bought him a warm coat and these sock type things to go over his paws as well as legwarmers, so he's having a blast in the gardens with Joe.'

'It's great that they're best friends.'

'Joe is crazy about Kismet, so I'm glad Ava convinced me to let him adopt a greyhound. Seeing them play together as well as snuggle on the sofa together makes me think I should have got him a dog ages ago.'

'Everything happens for a reason and when it's meant to, right?' I say the words and they make me think of my own circumstances and how fortunate it was that I bumped into Carla that night. If I hadn't, I don't know what she'd have done, and I'd have missed out on seeing what a delectable woman she's become.

'I'm thinking so,' Edward says. 'Anyway, I was asking if you have plans a week tomorrow because we're having our Christmas party at the house and we'd like you to come. Bring your guest if you like.'

His grin tells me he's keen to meet her and I suspect Ava is too. I'm the one out of us three friends who swore he'd never get involved and who makes sure that they rarely see me with the same woman twice, so I can't blame them for being keen to meet the woman who's been sharing my home. If the situation was reversed, I'd be keen to meet her too.

Something darts through my chest, and I take a deep breath. What was that? Was it jealousy? Do I want to keep Carla all to myself? Locked away in my apartment where no one can see or speak to her and where I can do all manner of wicked things to her and make her come over and over and over. The thought of her coming and how wet she gets makes my cock twitch so I adjust my position in the chair. Workplace erections are not at all convenient.

'So?' Edward is standing now and he picks up his papers and his iPad.

'I'll be there.'

'Alone?' He tilts his head.

'I'll ask Carla if she'd like to come and let you know.'

'Great.' Edward crosses to the glass door and opens it. 'Why don't you head home a bit early and pick up something nice for your mystery lady? Tell her we can't wait to meet her.'

'Sure.' Laughing, I get up and tuck the chair under the long polished table. It's a table that's seen many meetings, where we've discussed issues such as buying out other firms so we can take their contracts, where we've debated cutting jobs or raising salaries, where we've signed deals and clinked champagne glasses at the rise in the value of our company shares. It's been a core location in the inner workings of Cavendish Construction, but now, as I look down at the dark wooden surface, all I can think about is picking Carla up and laying her down on it then spreading her legs and eating out that sweet, tight little pussy.

And now my cock is hard, pressing against my trunks and begging to be taken home to Carla. I think Edward was right. It's time to head home to my lovely guest.

Chapter 16
Carla

Staring down at the photographs that have fallen to the floor, I bite my lip. The box has torn and I'll need to see if I can repair it because the last thing I want is for Lucas to think I was snooping. I kneel down and I spot a familiar face on one of the glossy rectangles so I pick it up, and sure enough, my teenaged brother grins out at me. Behind him, Lucas is staring into the distance towards the sea. Both are wearing T-shirts and shorts, their feet bare, their hair wind tousled. They must have been about fourteen or fifteen, their faces fresh and young, their skin tanned, their limbs long and wiry, not the full, muscular limbs they both have now. I can remember them being this way and something inside me twangs, like an elastic band being flicked. Where did the time go? Back then, we were all so innocent and unmarred by life. We had no idea what was coming next and, thankfully, no idea what life would bring or how quickly it would pass.

I shift to sit cross-legged on the carpet and set the photo aside, then reach for another. The box is like a treasure chest of photos of Lucas over the years and I browse them all, watching as Lucas goes from small child to teen to young boy and to man. I rarely print out photographs anymore as they're all in my iCloud storage, but I can see that having physical copies must have been so enjoyable. Of course, you can't enlarge them with your thumb and forefinger, nor can you tweak the lighting or the tones, but you can look at them again and again, even if your phone battery dies or your online storage crashes.

When I come to a photo with Lucas, Dane, and a girl, my breath catches in my throat. He has a photo of me! I'm around eleven and Lucas stands on one side of me, Dane on the other. We three smile at the camera, our cheeks flushed and eyes bright. Dane has his hand on my shoulder and Lucas is making rabbit ears behind my head. It makes me laugh. This is the Lucas I remember: a joker, a prankster, a bit of a tough guy at times. Even back then, I recall thinking he was cute and sophisticated. Older than me, he was out of reach, my brother's best friend, a boy who would never look my way, but that didn't stop me admiring him and wondering what it would be like if he kissed me. Lucas would have been around seventeen on this photo and he's still boyish but showing signs of the man he'll become. His shoulders are broadening, his upper lip shadowed with fluff, his jaw widening into the firm square jaw he has now. What did he think of me back then? That I was a child who trailed around after him when he came to our home, who asked him questions that bored him and who stuffed her bra with tissues to appear more grown up? There was a world of difference in our ages then, that gap between child and young adult that cannot be bridged. I send out a silent thank you to the universe that now, at twenty-nine and thirty-five, we no longer have a gap of any significance between us and can enjoy being together as two grown adults.

When I've finished browsing, I pack all the photographs neatly back in the box and set it on the bed, intending on searching for some tape to fix the side when I've finished organising. A ping from my phone on the dressing table sends me to check it, and when I see a text from Lucas, my heart jumps. I shouldn't be so happy that he's thought of me and yet I am. Knowing that I'm on his mind even though he's at work warms me right through, so I unlock my phone and read.

> **Dear Houseguest,**
> **I hope you're taking it easy. London is messy today, the melting snow dark and slushy in the gutters, the roads wet and grimy. The forecast says there's more on the way in the next few days though, so when it comes, I'll take you out to see London wearing her white, icy cloak.**
> **I'll be on my way home soon and I'll stop and pick up something for dinner. Let me know if you have a preference or if you're craving anything. Like me... ;-)**
> **See you shortly,**
> **L x**

I read the message through three times before replying.

> **Dear Host,**
> **I am pleased to report that I've finally reorganised my clothing and am about to**

**take a shower. I intend on getting all wet
and soapy… ;-)
I like most foods, so surprise me. I'm
sure you'll choose well.
Looking forward to seeing you.
C xx**

After I've sent the message, I decide to send him something to remember me by and so I unbutton my pyjama top and slide it off my left shoulder then snap a photo of my neck and shoulder, the swell of my breast just showing at the bottom of the screen. No one could tell it was me and it's just enough to tease him.

I wait, watching the screen, and when the three dots appear to show he's typing, my stomach flips over. Have I done too much? What if he's in a meeting?

Finally, after what feels like hours of waiting, the dots disappear and I stare at my phone, disappointment settling over me.

But then my phone pings with a photo and I almost drop it because there, in front of me, is Lucas' crotch. He's wearing those smart suit trousers, but there's an unmistakable bulge underneath them. Knowing what's underneath the material sends heat to my core.

Another ping brings a text from him.

**Minx!
Look at what you've done to me now. I
was about to leave the conference room
but as you can see, your photograph
made me hard, so I'll need to wait for my**

erection to go down. For this, Carla, I'll need to punish you when I get home because you're a very naughty girl. You think carefully about what you've done, and I'll come up with something suitable for when I return. I'm thinking you need at least three orgasms to remember who I am and what I am capable of. Do NOT use one of your vibrators on yourself to relieve any tension, because I want the pleasure of doing that to you myself. Think about what I'm going to do to you because I want that pussy soaking wet when I taste it.
Yours from the top of the rock (hard cock),
L xx

Now I drop my phone on the bed and cover my face with my hands. Something bubbles in my throat and emerges as a giggle. I'm so embarrassed and yet so turned on. Lucas is going to bury his head between my thighs tonight, and I want that more than anything right now. I have gone from being a shutdown, lonely widow to a wanton woman desperate for a man's touch. But not just any man. It is Lucas I want. Just the thought of him seeing me naked, of him touching me and kissing me and licking me turns me on so much that my clit throbs needily, but he told me not to touch myself and so I won't. When he come home later, I want to be ready to explode and so I will wait. Needy. Wet. Pulsing with desire.

Will he fuck me tonight? The anticipation is enough to make me almost come without being touched and so I decide the best thing I can do right now is take a long, cold shower and keep my mind off Lucas Barrett. That man has a hold on me and my pussy and right now, I don't want him to ever let go.

Chapter 17

Lucas

I stop and pick up sushi in Soho along with a bottle of sake then I hurry home, keen to get to Carla. Funny to be keen to get home to see a woman. I'm thinking with my cock but it doesn't matter; I want this woman and nothing is going to change that now.

When I reach the building, I get in the lift and it seems to take forever to reach my floor. As the doors open, I hurry inside, stripping off my coat, scarf and suit jacket and throwing them onto the sofa. I set the bags of food and sake on the kitchen counter, then look around.

Where is she? It's so quiet.

Is she sleeping? Changing? Naked on the bed?

My cock roars to life and I rub at the shaft, letting him know it won't be long now.

'Carla?'

'In my room.'

I head straight there and find the door ajar, so I enter and close my eyes briefly as I inhale her scent. How can a woman smell so good? I love that the room smells like her now, of vanilla and pomegranates and a hint of lily.

'Hey,' she says from the bed where she's lying on her side, head propped up on her hand.

'Hey.' My eyes travel from her head to her toes, taking in her red hair that falls over her shoulder and covers her breasts. From here, it looks like she's not wearing anything else up top. I can see the curve of her belly and the indent of her bellybutton and then a scrap of pink lace that teases me with a flash of the red hair at the apex of her thighs. And those thighs ... so soft and round... No fashionable thigh gap in sight. This woman has curves everywhere and I fucking love it.

'How was your day?' She takes her hair and pushes it over her shoulders and I moan involuntarily because now I can see those incredible breasts: full, round, topped with her rosy nipples.

'It's getting better by the second.' My voice is gruff with desire. I remove my tie and cross to the bed, then bend over her and roll her onto her back. I trail the tie from her feet, up her shins and over her thighs, moving it from one side to the other like a snake.

Carla sighs and shivers as the tie drifts over her thong, then up her belly and over her full breasts, teasing those hard nipples into perfect peaks.

'Put your hands above your head,' I say, and her eyes widen.

'W-what?'

'Don't make me ask you again. I warned you I was going to punish you.'

She hesitates for a fraction of a second, then she raises her hands and I watch as the movement lifts her breasts. My cock is pressing so hard against my trunks now that it's painful.

I straddle her and wrap the tie around her wrists, looping them together, and then I wind the rest of the tie through the gaps on the elaborately carved wooden headboard. Once it's fastened, I give it a tug, and it stays in place.

'Now I can do what I want with you.' I smile down at Carla and she licks her lips. 'Is that OK with you?'

She nods.

'You can tell me to stop at any time and I will. Got it?'

'Yes.' Her cheeks are flushed and her pupils dilated.

'Now let me look at you.'

Sitting back on my heels, I drink her in. She's a woman who should inspire paintings that would be hung in a gallery for centuries. People could admire her form, her beauty, her purity. Yes, that's what it is. Carla is pure in a way I've never thought about before. She's been married and probably with other men before her husband, but it's not that. She has this air of innocence about her and it makes me wonder if it's because she trusts people too easily. Or loves too easily. Does she give her heart away without thinking about the consequences?

I take her small feet in my hands and raise them to my

mouth, then I kiss the toes, nibble at their tips and watch as she wriggles on the bed, close to laughter.

'Your feet are ticklish?' I ask.

'A bit.'

'Good.' I run my tongue over the soles then suck at her toes, but this time she doesn't wriggle, she watches me, awe filling her grey eyes. Setting her legs back down on the bed, I push them apart and stroke her inner thighs, up and down, getting closer to her pink thong each time. 'What a pretty little thong.'

'I hoped you'd like it,' she says.

'I like what's underneath it more.'

'I'm g-glad,' she replies as I slip a finger under the side of the material and brush it over her mound.

'You're drenched.'

'I was thinking about you all day.'

'Good girl.'

I tickle her clit, rousing the bud until it's hard and swollen, then I dip my finger lower and between her folds until I find her opening. My finger teases her for a bit and she pulsates around me, raises her hips to take me deeper, so I pull my hand away. The disappointment in her eyes makes me smile and I straddle her again and climb up her body, then take hold of those incredible tits. Lowering my head, I suckle at them, fill my mouth with them and Carla writhes beneath me.

'Let me touch you,' she says.

Meeting her eyes, I shake my head. 'Not yet. You're in my control right now.'

I give her breasts one more suck each and then I kiss her on the mouth, softly at first before plundering her with my tongue. I fuck her mouth with my tongue the way I want to do with my cock and Carla wraps her legs around mine and pulls me against her. My erection presses against her sex through my trousers and trunks, so hard now it feels like it could rip through the material. Carla moans as she grinds against me and I keep kissing her, teasing us both, and then she cries out as she comes.

When she's done, she flops back onto the bed and gazes at me, confusion in her eyes. 'Sorry.'

'Why're you sorry?' Brushing hair from her cheek, I rest above her on my elbows.

'I came with my underwear on. And yours.' She laughs softly and I smile down at her.

'Don't be sorry for that. We have plenty of time to undress. Speaking of that ...'

Standing, I strip off my clothes, then lie on the bed next to her, facing her so my cock presses against her thigh.

'What now?' she asks.

'This.' Taking hold of her hips, I turn her onto her right side and lie behind her, then pull her against me and lift her left leg. Pulling the thong away from her pussy, I slip my erection between her flesh and the material and let it rest there. I'm so hard my cock is throbbing, so I move it against her, creating friction between the tight thong and her folds. It would be so easy to push inside her right now, but that's not what I want. Not yet. Reaching down, I grab hold of myself and I fist my cock, rub her juices all over it and pump hard. In front of me, Carla writhes because my hand is brushing against her and so I drop my cock and reach around then caress her clit, slide my fingers inside her and move them up and down until she comes over my fingers and her juices run down over my erection. When she stops moaning, I pull my cock out of her thong and grab myself again and press against her perfect bum cheeks, then finish the job I started. When I come over her ass, I groan and milk every last drop of cum out of my cock.

'I don't know about you, Carla, but I'm fucking starving now,' I murmur into her back.

'Me too.' She peers over her shoulder at me and smiles almost shyly. 'That was so hot.'

After I've rolled her onto her back, I sit up and untie her hands, then bring them down to her sides and kiss her tenderly.

The look in her eyes fractures something inside me, so I pull her into my arms and hold her tight, nothing but a scrap of pink lace between us. Nothing, that is, other than the reason I can't fall in love with her and why, I think, I've been holding back from fucking her. Once I do, my feelings towards her might change. I might get bored, and I don't want to do that to her. Carla is the sexiest woman I have ever met. She is also the only woman I have wanted so badly that I'm prepared to wait. The only woman I don't want to get bored with.

I don't understand what's happening to me...

Chapter 18
Carla

The next afternoon, bundled up in my coat, hat, and gloves, I tramp out the lounge to find Lucas reading his phone at the kitchen island. He looks serious so I don't disturb him. Instead, I go to the window and peer out at the grey morning. It's cloudy but I can see down to the street and the roofs of the shorter buildings. The snow has stopped but there's evidence of it everywhere and more has been forecast. After Lucas untied me last night, we cuddled for a while and he held me so tight I could barely breathe. In his arms, I felt safe and cared for and incredibly sated after the orgasms he gave me. I'm not sure why he didn't penetrate me, but I'm sure there's a reason. Perhaps he just likes the anticipation of waiting and I have to admit that I'm enjoying it too. It's like being a horny teenager again and I suspect that when he does actually enter me, it will be amazing.

We dozed for a while in each other's arms, then dressed in our robes and came out to the lounge and ate the sushi he'd brought and washed it down with sake. Once we'd eaten our fill, we curled up on the sofa and finished the sake while watching a news programme that I found dry but that Lucas said had some relevance to a work project. I didn't even mind because I was cuddled up to him, full of food and relaxed after the intense foreplay.

Today we are heading out and I'm pretty excited about it because I can't remember the last time I explored a city with a man. Well, I can but it was completely different and I will not dwell on that now. I will be here and present in the moment and enjoy all that Lucas and London have to offer. This is all temporary, so I want to make the most of it while I can.

WE EXIT the apartment building in Mayfair and the cold air hits me instantly, making me shiver. It's a shock to my system after so long indoors and I press my lips together to protect my sensitive teeth.

'Be careful because there's some ice around.' Lucas takes my arm and I'm glad because the last thing I want now is to fall head over heels and injure myself.

I smile my thanks at Lucas, and a flash of desire rushes through me. He's wearing a grey wool beanie, a black coat, jeans, and lace up walking boots and he looks so handsome this morning. His stubble has grown. I can see the grey more clearly at this length and it gives him a distinguished air. Some days I catch myself wondering at how we've both aged. Not having seen him for so long means I missed out on him ageing and that thought can leave me a bit sad, but then I tell myself that it's life and this happens. Time waits for no one and it keeps moving forwards, ageing us one day at a time. That's for the lucky ones anyway because, as I know all too well, not everyone gets the luxury of time. Not everyone gets to grow old.

We tramp along the pavements, our breath huffing out before us like clouds of steam. The pavements are clear but snow lies in the gutter, melting, turned grey and brown by the dirt and debris of this vibrant city. In that respect, it's similar to New York because the snow there falls soft and pure white but soon gets tainted by pollution and people, just like life, I guess. None of us escape unscathed, but that's OK; it's part of the human experience to be changed by the world and all that happens to us during our lives. I wonder what has happened to Lucas over the years and what has changed him.

'Do you want to take the tube?' Lucas asks, pointing at sign for the underground.

Shaking my head, I smile. 'I'm happy to walk. After being indoors for a week, it's nice to be outside again.'

It takes about half an hour to get to Covent Garden, and when we reach the location, I get a shiver down my spine. It's simply breath-taking. There's a week and a half until Christmas and the historic site is as festive as it gets with Christmas trees, enormous baubles, hundreds of thousands of lights and a sprinkling of actual snow to complement it all.

We stroll around the traffic-free Piazza, and I feel like a child as we admire the decorations, the lights, the pop-ups and the giant Christmas tree. 'It's beautiful,' I say, and Lucas gives my arm a squeeze.

'I forget sometimes how amazing it is because I live in London and see it every year, but yes, it's quite spectacular.'

We reach the South Hall and come across the iconic red sleigh. A few people are queuing for photographs, and I pause.

'Would you like to have a photograph in the sleigh?' Lucas asks.

'No, it's fine.' Shaking my head, I go to walk away, but Lucas catches my elbow.

'Come on. Let's do it.'

So we wait our turn and then Lucas helps me to climb up into the carriage and I sit, expecting him to take a photo of me with his phone, but he doesn't. Instead, he speaks into the ear of a man standing nearby then hands him his phone. Next thing I know, he's sitting at my side with his arm around my waist. He gazes at me and there's something in his eyes that makes my heart race. When he leans closer and presses a soft kiss to my lips, my breath catches and I sigh against him, then cuddle in as we smile at the camera.

As Lucas helps me down from the sleigh, the man hands him his phone, then says, 'You make a lovely couple. How long have you been together?'

Lucas winks at me. 'A long time, but it feels like mere days.'

'That's true love for you,' the man says. 'It always feels like you're at the beginning, even when you've been together for years. Hope you have a wonderful Christmas together.'

'Thank you,' I reply then Lucas takes my hand and we walk away.

We stop in front of a stall, and Lucas gets his wallet out. 'Mulled wine?'

'Yes please.'

While he orders some wine, I look around, thinking about what the man had said. This time last year, my life was so different. I had no idea I'd be widowed, that I'd have to leave my home and return to the UK. I had no idea about the pain I was about to experience and how it would consume me. Some days I felt empty, like I had nothing left to give and like I could simply curl up, shutdown and cease to exist. People told me that time would heal, but I don't think it does. Time moves you away from your loss but it doesn't heal so much as give you the opportunity to grow around your grief. You become accustomed to living with it and you put one foot in front of the other and keep going. There's no easy fix and no one can do your grieving for you. People can be kind, they can say and do things to show that they care, but no one can ever take the pain away. Time can't even do that. It's still early days, I know that, but I can't imagine ever not feeling the wave of loss that sweeps through me when I think of calling Kofi to ask what I fancy for dinner. When his favourite song comes on the radio, and I think about him dancing around the apartment holding a wooden spoon and pretending to sing into it. When I recall holding him close through the winter nights when our heating was on the blink and we'd snuggle closer for warmth, my face buried in his neck, my feet cold even in socks, tucked between his legs. He was my best friend for so long, my person, the one who was always going to be there for me throughout life and then, suddenly, he was gone. How can anyone ever get over that type of loss? And god, the loneliness, the terrible all-consuming loneliness of losing your person is just beyond comprehension. Even now, it's so enormous that it makes my chest tight and threatens to push me into insanity. But this thing I have with Lucas, temporary as it might be, is helping me to feel things other than the choking agony of loss. It's helping me to connect with my body again and to be me — not a widow, not alone, not bereft. Lucas has come into my life at a time when I needed someone to hold me, kiss me and make love to me and I can't help feeling that this was meant to happen now. Why else would I have bumped into him after so long in a bar on a snowy night when I had nowhere else to go? Something, or someone, was looking out for me and brought Lucas to me like a knight in shining armour when I needed him most. I am so grateful to the universe for the gift of him. This Christmas, my first as a widow, will be hard enough, but having Lucas there will help and so I am making the most of this time with him.

When he returns to my side, he's carrying two recyclable cups of wine and he hands me one. I inhale the delicious scents of cinnamon and cloves, of orange and berries. It tastes even better and as the alcohol hits my stomach; I relax a bit more and smile at this wonderful man in front of me.

'What is it?' he asks.

'What do you mean?'

'That look you're giving me.' His blue eyes tease me.

'I'm just happy to be here with you.'

'Me too.' He nods. 'It's good to have company and I'm enjoying seeing London through fresh eyes. I think I've become a bit jaded with working so hard and ... ahem ... playing hard, and I know I'm guilty of taking things like

Covent Garden for granted. But being here with you is teaching me to slow down and smell the roses, as they say.'

'Do you think you're jaded?' I sip my wine, savour the spice and citrus of the hot drink.

'I can be. It's all too easy to get that way when you're a workaholic who doesn't have many real relationships.'

'With women?' The question makes my stomach tighten because I hate to think of him with other women, even though I'm sure he's had plenty. He's gorgeous, wealthy and sophisticated, so why wouldn't he have women falling over themselves to be with him?

'Yeah ... with women, but also with other people.'

'What about your family?' I remember little about his parents, only that he spent a lot of time at our house or out with Dane.

A small line appears between his dark brows and a muscle twitches in his jaw. 'Shall we finish these and have a wander?'

The way he deflects my question makes me want to ask more, but I saw the darkness in his eyes when I asked about his family, so I think it's best I leave it for now. I don't want to ruin today by bringing anything into it that upsets him.

'I have something else planned for us this afternoon.' He drains his wine so I do the same, then he drops the cups into the recycling bin near the stall and takes my hand again.

'What? Where are we going?'

'Wait and see.'

Chapter 19

Lucas

We leave Covent Garden and I hail a black cab, then whisper our destination to the driver. I booked an activity for this evening and hope Carla will enjoy herself.

We sit together in the back of the cab and Carla gazes out of the window, watching as the landmarks of central London fly past. I'm still holding her hand and it's like I can't let go. This isn't me at all, but there's something about Carla that makes me want to protect her. *Even from my past?* Yes, I think so. I hate thinking about my childhood and how things were back then because it brings a whole load of horrid feelings to the surface and, to be honest, I'd really prefer to leave them buried. What's the point in dwelling on the past and things I can't change? What is it they say? Look forward and leave your past in the rear-view mirror? You can't change yesterday, but you can change tomorrow? Besides which, the vulnerability in Carla that I suspect is linked to her ex irks me. I figure that helping her to enjoy her time with me will hopefully take her mind off the reason for the sadness I catch in her eyes now and then. The thought that perhaps her ex was abusive has occurred to me more than once and it's a thought that makes my blood boil. If he did hurt her, then I want to find out where he is right now and give him a taste of his own medicine. Domestic violence is loathsome to me and thinking that some cowardly shit might have hurt Carla makes me want to hunt him down and tear him limb from limb. This beautiful, gentle woman should never feel sad or afraid and I want to ensure that it never happens again. She's entitled to feel safe and secure, happy and free, and I'll do everything in my power to ensure that she does. I already feel responsible for her and that she's in my care, so it's only natural for me to want to keep her safe.

But how will I do that when she leaves me and goes back to Devon? How can I protect her then?

Make her mine...

The thought startles me and I sit back against the seat of the cab and take a shaky breath. *Mine? Make her mine? But how?* Would she even want to be mine? We agreed this would be temporary and I never thought for a moment that it would lead to deeper feelings, but with every day that Carla stays with me, it gets harder to remind myself that this will pass. Come January, Carla will leave; her beautiful body and lovely company will only be mine to enjoy for a brief time.

I could ask her to stay longer, ask for more than we've agreed, but if I do that I risk bringing my darkness to Carla and tainting her with it. I don't want that for her because there are things inside of me that no one should ever see or have to deal with. I'm broken inside and it's why I bury myself in work and women, why I keep busy so I don't have to stop and think about things I've felt in the past. Carla deserves better than me and what I have to offer and so as much as I want to protect her long-term, I can't. I am the demon she needs to be protected from and while I can enjoy this temporary fling we're having, anything more permanent would be bad for her. Carla deserves the world and I am not the man to give it to her.

When the cab pulls up at the location, I pay the driver, then get out and hold out my hand for Carla. She takes it and smiles when she sees where we are.

'How are you on skates?' I ask.

'Not the best.' She laughs. 'I went skating in Central Park last Christmas and...' She bites her lips and a frown mars her beautiful brow.

'And?' My jaw clenches as I see that sadness in her eyes again and imagine getting the address of her ex and jumping on the first flight out to JFK.

Carla lowers her gaze and stares at her boots for a moment and when she looks back up, it's like a shutter has come down over her face and she's a different person. 'And nothing. Well, just that I wasn't very good.' She waves a hand dismissively. 'Still ... perhaps I'll be better now. But surely we won't get in without a booking?'

'All taken care of.' I grin, because having money opens doors to restaurants, ice skating sessions and more. Even if I make last-minute plans, I can usually wangle anything I want with a flash of a credit card and a promise of a favour returned. I figure it doesn't hurt anyone and so I do use my money and status to open doors that would otherwise remain closed. When I thought about what I'd like to do with Carla today, ice skating was one of the things that came to mind, so I made a call and now we have tickets to hit the ice. Well, not *hit* the ice, I hope, but to enjoy some time together skating. 'The ice awaits, my lady.'

I hold out my hand and Carla takes it then we head towards Battersea Power Station together.

Chapter 20
Carla

Walking towards the power station, I experience a mixture of excitement and nerves. I'm not great on ice skates, I wasn't lying about that, and the thought of skating fills me with unease but I don't want to ruin Lucas' plans by being a spoilsport so I'll grit my teeth and hope for the best. I don't have the best balance on dry land, so being on ice is not something I'd choose to do, but Lucas looked so enthusiastic about it. Anyway, perhaps I'll be better this time. *And pigs could fly...*

The grade II listed building is an incredible sight, with its tall chimneys and proximity to the Thames. I remember my father telling me about the history of the place and how it once supplied a fifth of London's electricity, then lay derelict for decades. Now it's a thriving centre for new generations to shop, eat and skate and to while away the time while enjoying everything it now offers.

'It's so festive,' I say as we approach the front of the building with its amazing views of the Thames. There are three interconnecting rinks surrounded by twinkling lights, and an enormous Christmas tree.

'It's wonderful how they renovated this entire area.' Lucas squeezes my hand. 'We would have loved the contract, but it was highly coveted and Cavendish Construction lost out. But that's business for you: win some, lose some.'

Once we've checked in at the desk and swapped our shoes for ice-skates, my stomach is tight with nerves. I try to stand but the boots feel heavy and awkward on my feet, so Lucas takes my hands and helps me up. We plod over to the clear plastic side of the rink and he places my hands on it.

'I'm not sure now,' I say, annoyed at myself for being cowardly, but suddenly the thought of falling on the ice fills me with dread.

'Look ... why don't I go on first and let you have a breather, then I'll come back and get you? If you really don't want to skate, you don't have to.' His smile reassures me, so I nod and he lets himself through the gate and onto the ice. 'Back soon!'

And then he's off, gliding over the ice like he owns it, his feet moving with confidence, his handsome face wearing the biggest smile. He twists and turns and skates with speed and agility and my admiration for him grows. I had no idea he could skate, but then why would I? We haven't seen each other in years and so there's a lot I don't know about him. For such a big man, he's so elegant and graceful, and I know that I'm no match for him and how wonderful he is. Lucas and I are so different and he's just ... spectacular. In many ways, I'm still the little frumpy little sister with braces and puppy fat and a huge crush on the gorgeous older boy.

When I see him returning to where I'm waiting, my mouth goes dry. I can't do this, I really can't.

'How're you feeling?' he asks, holding my gaze with those bright blue eyes. His cheeks are flushed and he looks so full of life, so delightfully alive.

'OK.' I swallow against the parched feeling in my mouth.

'Fancy a go?'

'All right.' He's gone to the trouble of bringing me here, so the least I can do is make an effort.

Shuffling to the gate, my ankles feeling like glass, I wait while he opens it, then grip hold of his hand and step onto the ice. At first, it's not too bad and I move my feet bit by bit while he closes the gate then takes both my hands in his.

He skates backwards, holding my hands, and I glide along. Having Lucas hold me tight and support me as we do this gives me new confidence and I laugh as we sail forwards. Lucas glances behind him occasionally to ensure he doesn't crash into anyone, and I allow myself to lower my shoulders and relax.

'I'm actually enjoying this,' I say, and Lucas' smile is a reward that warms me right through. He pulls me towards him and wraps me in his embrace and we stand still for a moment, heart to heart, body to body, human to human. Being with Lucas makes me feel alive, and that's something to treasure because life is so fragile that we never know how long we've got.

When he releases me and leaves me standing alone, panic engulfs me and I wobble, but then he's behind me, his left hand on my waist and the other holding my right hand. His arm is around my back so I can lean on him and, once again, I feel safe. He won't let me fall, I know he won't and so as he starts to move us; I relax into him and glide along.

The air is cold against my cheeks, the lights twinkle all around us and the atmosphere is magical. Christmas songs play and I experience a spark of the magic of Christmas that I always used to feel. It was my favourite time of year as a child and then as an adult. New York was always beautiful at Christmas, even when we didn't have much money for gifts or decorations. For me, it was about being with my husband and having some precious time together, watching old movies and drinking hot chocolates while eating mince pies I made using my grandmother's recipe. Simple things are so precious.

As the grief lurches in my chest, I tilt my head and peer up at Lucas and he smiles, then leans down and kisses my cheek. It's a gentle kiss, but it sends heat to my core and banishes the looming pain. This man is helping me to heal without even knowing that he's doing it and with each passing day, he gets under my skin a little bit more. This might be temporary, but it will always remain in my heart as one of the good times in life that I can cling to during the darker days.

Lucas is everything I never knew I needed and while it breaks my heart that Kofi is in my past, I know I can cling to Lucas in the present, and that's all that matters for now. I cannot allow anything else to matter in this moment because it will be my undoing and if I let it all in, then I will unravel completely and nothing will be able to put me back together again.

Chapter 21

Lucas

Holding Carla on the ice did something funny to my heart. She's a strong and resilient woman, but there's something below the surface that's shaky and it gets to me. I've never felt like this before about a woman and I'm sure it's because I knew her years ago. It's like she's a link to the past and it makes me want to be nicer to her than I would usually be towards a woman. I feel compelled to take care of her, and make her feel special during her time with me. Doesn't she, above everyone, deserve to feel that she's treasured?

After we returned our ice skates, we wandered around the area for a bit while we decided what we wanted to eat. We settled on tapas and so now we're in a corner booth of a tapas restaurant at Battersea Power Station. It's warm and cosy and we're sitting close, our knees brushing against each other every time either of us moves. We're sipping cocktails, a mezcalita for her and an old-fashioned for me, and to eat we've ordered a selection of dishes to share. The restaurant is busy but in the corner booth I secured with a discreet tip, we're away from the hustle and bustle and have some privacy.

'So how come you skate so well?' Carla asks, her grey eyes meeting mine. Her red hair tumbles over her shoulders and brushes her breasts in the navy long sleeved top she's wearing. A flash of desire shoots through me as I think about how gorgeous those breasts are naked.

'I thought I told you.'

'Nope. Not in any detail, anyway.'

'I played ice hockey at university.'

'Did you?' She smiles. 'Were you good?'

Giving a small shrug, I laugh. 'I was OK. It wasn't at professional level or anything, but I did learn to skate well. You kind of have to be able to stand up on the ice and to move quickly when you're playing a game. It was good exercise and fun but I wouldn't want to do it these days. Not at my age.'

'You're not old.' She shakes her head.

'Getting there though.' I wink at her to show I'm teasing. 'I'm heading towards forty and I don't fancy the injuries that can come with playing ice hockey. It's a rough game.'

'I'm sure it is. I've seen some of the fights that occur. My husband used to watch it on TV. And go to the occasional game.'

Her expression falters and I see that darkness in her eyes again. that makes me want to press her for details. But then I know those details might make me want to hunt her husband down and destroy him, so ...

'Did you go with him?' I ask.

'Once or twice, but it wasn't really my thing and our work patterns often clashed, anyway.'

'What does he do?'

'Teach.'

I nod and try to hide my surprise. No man who upsets a woman the way he seemed to have upset Carla should be anywhere near children.

'And you were working for a charity and at a hotel?'

'In the HR department and as a cleaner at the hotel.'

'Sounds like you were busy.'

'Yeah.' Carla takes a drink and then another, and I understand that she wants the conversation to move on. Luckily, at that moment our food arrives and so we wait until the server has gone before speaking again.

'This looks good,' I say.

'It looks delicious.'

We've ordered a variety of dishes and my mouth waters as I look at the Gordal olives hand-stuffed with orange, chillies, and oregano; Iberico ham croquets; anchovies marinated in garlic, chilli, and parsley; patatas bravas; garlic and chilli fried king prawns and rare strips of chimichurri sirloin steak.

While we eat, I glance at Carla from time to time, watching how she savours each mouthful and gently dabs at her full lips with her napkin. When I see that her drink is almost gone, I order another round, and she smiles at me, making my heart leap in my chest in a way that reminds me of being at the highest point of a rollercoaster track then dropping over the edge. The worrying thing is that I could get used to feeling like this and it scares me because this can't last. There's no way we can get past my darkness and yet, I catch myself wishing every now and then, that there was.

Chapter 22

Carla

The food is so good that I eat and eat, my tongue tingling from the chillies and garlic, and I know my breath is going to stink later and tomorrow but it's so good I don't care. At least Lucas is eating the same things so hopefully we'll cancel each other out in terms of garlic breath.

'Why're you smiling?' he asks.

'I didn't realise I was.' My cheeks flush at the thought of sharing my musings with him.

'Tell me what you're thinking.'

'It's kind of embarrassing.'

'Try me.'

'OK then. I was thinking ... that our breath is going to stink, but then I thought that we'll both smell the same so perhaps we won't notice.'

Lucas laughs, his head thrown back, his straight white teeth on display. He doesn't laugh like that often and it's good to see, like he's relaxed enough with me now to laugh in that way.

'We'll have to test out your theory later then, won't we?'

The look in his blue eyes makes a shiver run down my spine. I know that look now and it means that he's got one thing on his mind and he's going to do what he wants to me later. He'll make me feel better than I dreamt I could ever feel again. Between my legs, my clit pulses and I press my thighs together to give the hard nub some friction.

'In fact, I wonder where you'll taste of garlic, Carla. How quickly will it travel through your bloodstream? If I kiss your neck, will I taste it there? If I suckle your nipples, will the chilli tingle my lips? If I go lower ... and push your thighs apart then lick your cunt, will you taste of garlic there? Will the chilli on my tongue make your sweet clit tingle?'

I can barely swallow now because of the heat rushing through my veins. Something tells me that this discussion about garlic and chilli shouldn't be so hot and yet it is because I'm thinking about Lucas' mouth on my skin, his teeth grazing my nipples and his hot tongue between my legs. God this man can arouse me in ways I didn't know were possible.

'Shall we order dessert to go?' he asks and I nod, unable to reply.

He drains his glass, then signals to the server and soon, he settles the bill and a small brown cardboard box containing dessert is placed on the table. We don our coats, hats, and gloves then head out into the chill of the late afternoon, but despite the icy wind, I am warm inside because Lucas has set me aglow.

Chapter 23

Carla

The return journey to the apartment is a blur. Lucas held my hand as we walked, placed a hand on my knee in the cab, wrapped an arm around my shoulders as we rode the lift to his penthouse. The air between us fizzed with anticipation and as soon as we entered the apartment, I knew tonight would be special.

'Get undressed,' he says, his tone filled with authority.

I stand before him and remove my coat, hat and gloves, then my boots, top and jeans. When I'm down to my turquoise lace bra and panties, his eyes appraise me, something primal in his proprietorial gaze. He wants me and it makes me feel powerful, feminine, and whole.

'Now you,' I say and he raises his brows slowly.

He strips off quickly, tossing his clothing aside until he stands before me in just his jeans. His body is so gorgeous I could weep. From his broad shoulders to his sculpted chest and toned abs, the Adonis belt that leads down to his waistband, encouraging me to gaze at his groin, and the bulge that strains against the denim, he is masculinity personified. I bite my bottom lip as a shiver of lust clenches at my core and I know that more than anything, I want Lucas for dessert.

'What about the rest?' I lift a brow in question.

'Not yet.' He holds my gaze while he undoes his belt and slides it out of his jeans, then stalks towards me. He takes my hand and leads me to the lounge area and I go to sit on the sofa, but he shakes his head. 'Lie on the table.'

I look at the low coffee table and frown.

'Lie down.'

I sit on the coffee table then lie back. The marble is cold against my skin and my nipples pebble while goosebumps rise all over my body.

Lucas towers over me with desire written all over his face. He crouches at the end of the table, then pushes my thighs apart so they're either side of the table legs. I lie there as he wraps the belt around my left ankle, then round the table leg and does the same on the other side before fastening the belt. My legs are now held fast, my thighs spread, and Lucas stares down at the flimsy material of my panties that is already exposing the outer lips of my sex.

'Fucking beautiful,' he says. 'Take off your bra.'

I lift my head and reach around under my back and undo the clasp, then slide the garment down my arms and Lucas takes it. He slides the one strap over my left wrist, then bends over and slides the bra strap under the table top before slipping the other strap around my right arm so my arms are pinned at my sides. I'm now held fast and couldn't move if I wanted to.

'Are you comfortable, Carla?'

I think about it. Am I? Not really because the marble is cold and hard and my head is almost hanging off the end of the table, but I also don't mind. I feel alive. I am more conscious of my body than my mind right now and that is a welcome escape.

'I guess so.'

'You guess so?'

He walks around the table slowly until he's standing behind my head, leans over and runs his hands over my belly, stroking slowly circles around my bellybutton and then upwards between my breasts. Suddenly, he places both hands over my breasts and cups them before pinching my nipples hard enough to make me gasp. 'How does that feel?' His voice is low, dangerous.

'So good,' I whisper.

He pinches again and my back arches of its own accord, pushing my breasts into his hands and he cups them, ducks his head and sucks at my nipples in turn.

'I'll be back in a moment.'

He leaves my side and I lie there, my chest rising rapidly, wondering what he's going to do next. I hear his footsteps retreat, then return and the rustle of the box from the tapas restaurant opening. And then he's back, his impressive frame at my feet.

'You can stop me at any time. Just tell me to stop and I will. Understand?'

I nod. My heart is racing and I couldn't speak if I wanted to.

'Close your eyes.'

I do and then I feel him slip something down over my head and adjust my hair so it falls from the table behind me. He's so gentle at times that I could weep. Now blindfolded, I hold my breath for a moment so I can listen to him.

'Relax now Carla because I am going to serve dessert.'

A clink of metal against glass.

The sensation of him straddling the table, his legs either side of me.

And then something cold being smeared in a line from my throat to my belly and over my nipples. When he tugs at my panties I hear the fabric tearing and his grunt of approval. 'I'll replace these,' he says. 'Now lie very still and don't make a sound.'

His hot breath tickles the shells of my ears and then his tongue caresses my skin, moving tantalisingly slowly down the trail he left on my body, pausing at my nipples to suck hard. With each suck, my core spasms as he stimulates the link between nipple and womb and I bite my lip hard not to cry out.

When his mouth moves lower, I wriggle, anticipating when I'll feel his mouth on my sex and I don't have to wait long. He lathers his tongue over my mound, then pushes it between the folds, running it in a figure of eight over my clit. The pressure builds and I yearn for him to fill me, so when he inserts two large fingers, I push up onto them, keen to feel them stretching me.

Without my sight, I am all about sensation, and I feel everything as he hooks the two fingers and stimulates my G-spot while he goes to town on my clit. As he suckles the hard nub and works his fingers inside me, I climb higher and higher, my body consumed by sensation and then, when I am at the peak, my body contracting around his fingers he says, 'You can speak now, sweeting.'

I let out a roar of ecstasy as I barrel over the edge of the abyss and the orgasm consumes me, pulsing at my core and echoing throughout my body, so I bounce against his fingers, keen to squeeze every last tingle of pleasure. When I am done, I flop exhausted against the table and feel Lucas give my tender pussy one last slow, lingering kiss.

'Time for you to have some chocolate mousse, Carla,' he says and I lick my lips.

'That's it sweeting. Lubricate those lips for me and get them as wet as your pussy, just the way I like it.'

I hear him drop his jeans to the floor and kick them away and then his trunks. The mousse pot clinks as it's set on the floor and then his knees brush against my shoulders. His hands take hold of me under my armpits and he pulls me higher up the table so my head hangs off the edge.

When he kisses my lips, I sigh against him and then he kisses all along my jaw and back to my mouth. When he frees my arms and places my hands behind his knees, I feel the hair on his calves and the heat of his skin.

'If you need me to stop, tap my leg.'

'Yes.'

Something touches my lips, and I part them and taste chocolate. I stick out my tongue and am rewarded with more.

'Eat my cock, baby,' Lucas growls and then he pushes the tip into my mouth. I suck at him, roll my tongue over the tip of him and taste the salty pre-cum mixed in with the chocolate mousse. He slides deeper with each thrust and so I push my head back and take him down my throat, breathing through my nose and creating a channel for him to fill. 'That's the way, Carla, keep going.'

He pumps in and out and my jaw aches with the effort of taking all of him, but I won't stop. I want to swallow him whole.

His cock swells and then he tenses. There's a brief moment, mere seconds before his heat spurts down my throat and I swallow greedily, milking every last drop of semen from him to show him how much I desire him and want him inside me.

We stay still for a moment, our hearts slowing down, our bodies still joined then he pulls out gently. He kisses my lips and I push my tongue into his mouth, wanting to share his taste with him and he moans against me.

'I fucking love tasting you, Carla,' he says.

When he removes the blindfold, I squint against the lamp-light, and he gently caresses my face, then gets up and goes around to my legs and unties them. He helps me to sit up and my legs shake, but he scoops me up and lays me down on the sofa and covers me with a soft throw.

Starting Over With the Billionaire

'I'll get us a drink,' he says and I watch as he walks away, his firm ass cheeks one of the best things I've ever seen.

I lie back, wincing at the way my thighs ache after being held apart for so long, but I'm smiling. I never imagined I'd like being tied up or dominated. This is no extreme play, but it's erotic and very different to what I've experienced in the past. Kofi was always a gentle lover, quite vanilla, and it worked for us. But I like how Lucas takes charge and does what he wants with me. It makes me feel feminine and desired and I can surrender to my physical needs and let him please me while he takes his own pleasure.

As of yet, we haven't had penetrative sex, but I'm sure that when we do, it will be every bit as incredible as everything else we've done so far. I can hardly wait...

Chapter 24

Carla

The next week flies past with Lucas at work most days and me at the apartment. I rest, watch some TV, soak in the tub and pamper myself in ways I haven't done in what feels like a lifetime. It is, quite simply, glorious. On the second day alone, I venture out, smiling at the security guard as I leave, aware that he must be curious about who I am, and then set off to explore. I wander around the area, admire the architecture, take some photos on my old phone and then do some food shopping. I thought it would be nice to make Lucas dinner to thank him for having me stay and for his kindness and so I pick up some different meats and vegetables, some fresh pasta, and herbs and a few bottles of fine wine. Lucas enjoys coming home to a meal so much that I do it every day when he's been at work and the rewards, apart from his gorgeous smile, have been many orgasms in lots of different positions. It's like we're enjoying a long round of foreplay that's lasting deliciously, and sooner or later — please be sooner — it will result in mind blowing sex!

This evening we are off to Lucas' friend's Christmas party and I'm nervous about meeting his friend and his wife but also excited about seeing where they live and how they live. Already, Lucas' wealth has amazed me and it's clear that he doesn't have to scrimp and save, which is so different from my life back in New York when we had to watch every cent. Lucas has money. I don't know exactly what kind of money other than that it's a lot. I mean, I looked up the apartment on a website that tells you how much it went for and we're talking millions for a place like this and that's just the shell. Add in the fixtures and fittings, the furniture, and furnishings and you're talking super expensive. Of course, that made me think of Kofi and how hard he worked as a teacher and what he'd have thought about all this. If he'd had an easier life with fewer hours at work, would he still be here? If we'd been able to afford to eat better quality food, would he still be waking up next to me every morning and not gone forever?

In the bedroom, I brush my hair in front of the mirror then smooth some serum through it to stop it frizzing up. I can't deny that I look better than when I arrived in London just over two weeks ago. My face is not as gaunt, my eyes not as haunted, and the dark shadows beneath them have gone. It's amazing the effect that being here with Lucas has had upon me. He's healing me and I'll always be grateful to him for that.

'Knock! Knock!' He peeps around the open doorway. 'All right to come in?'

'Of course.'

I tuck my long-sleeved white top into my high-waisted jeans and push my hair behind my ears.

'You're looking particularly beautiful this morning,' Lucas says. We slept separately again last night because he said he often gets up with insomnia and doesn't want to wake me. I have to agree with him because after not sleeping well for months, it's a relief to get six or seven unbroken hours.

'I feel good, thank you.' Smiling, I cross the room and he opens his arms as naturally as if we've been doing this every day for years. He smells like summer rain in the woods and I breathe him in, savour the feeling of his strong arms around me. It will be so hard to leave this behind and I am going to miss him, but for now, I don't have to worry about that. Something hard pokes into my belly, and I tilt my head to look up at him. 'It seems that you're feeling good, too.' I giggle and he grins.

'Yeah, you seem to have this effect upon me. I'd love to do something about it but we need to head out.'

'We do?'

'We have an appointment.'

'Oh?'

'I'll explain when we get there.'

Nodding, I reach for my jacket and hat and follow him out into the hallway.

'I hope you're going to like it.' He holds my gaze and something passes between us that makes my heart squeeze. Sometimes it seems like he has something he wants to say and then the moment passes and I'm left wondering about what it could possibly be. But then, as human beings, we often fail to say things even when we should know better because we cannot guarantee tomorrow.

We leave the building and Lucas points at a limousine parked at the kerb, the driver standing next to the open door. 'Your chariot awaits, my lady.'

'We're travelling in style.' I slide into the back seat and gaze around me, admiring the finery of the vehicle. Lucas gets in and comes closer to me and takes my hand.

'You should always travel in style, Carla.'

Embarrassed, I look away, because if only he knew how poor I have been and how I often had to take the bus or subway in New York, how a limousine was the stuff of dreams and never a vehicle I would have thought to travel in. The luxury is incredible and yet overwhelming and I'd like to ask Lucas how he got used to it. I don't remember him having much money growing up, but then he went to Oxford on a scholarship and has been working in the construction business since he graduated, so I'm guessing he's accustomed to it now. Money opens doors and raises people up, and it's definitely that way with him. And yet, it doesn't seem to have tarnished him. Yes, he could be an idiot at times when we were younger, but then perhaps he was dealing with things that I didn't know about or understand. We were essentially children back then, and a lot has changed over the years.

The limo moves through the streets of London and it's like we're in a bubble because I can't hear a thing from outside. The noise and pollution is out there but in here we are safe and warm, sitting on fine leather seats as soft as butter and Lucas is still holding my hand, tracing circles on my palm with his fingers. He does this almost absently now, as if it's natural for him, and it soothes me to be touched by him like this.

Christmas lights twinkle on lampposts and the fronts of buildings, trees sway in the breeze, making their fairy lights dance like fireflies and everywhere I look there is colour and festive joy. London at Christmas is remarkable and I'm happy to be here with Lucas and to experience this during my first Christmas without Kofi. Had I been in New York in our apartment, it would have been unbearable, and so I am glad to have this time out, this time to gather my strength and begin moving on with my life.

When the limo stops and the driver gets out, I wait until the door opens and Lucas slides along the seat, then he reaches for me. In front of us in the iconic Harrods building and I gaze at its glorious festive displays and thousands of twinkling lights. Snow sits on the corners of the windowsills and on the ground outside the building, while inside, festive scenes play out.

'Come on.' Lucas waves at the driver, then leads me inside.

It's another world — enormous, glittering, fragranced with cinnamon and pine. There is colour everywhere I look, and Lucas laughs as he watches me taking it all in.

'What are we doing here?' I ask.

'Some shopping.' He raises my hand and kisses it, then we head through the store.

When we reach the womenswear department, a tall, angular woman with dark hair pulled into a tight bun on the top of her head approaches us and Lucas shakes her hand.

'Mr Barrett, it's good to see you.'

'Good to see you too, Arabella,' Lucas says, then turns to me. 'This is Carla.'

The woman appraises me in what feels like an assessment but then she smiles, and it reaches her hazel eyes. 'Hello, Carla, and welcome to the Harrods personal shopping service. I'll be assisting you today. What is it you're looking for?'

I open my mouth to answer, but I don't know and so I turn to Lucas.

'Carla and I are heading to a Christmas party this evening, so she needs a dress, shoes, and accessories.'

While he speaks, Arabella types into an iPad, her long lashes fluttering beneath wide black brows that I suspect are tattooed on.

Lucas sounds so sure of himself and his confidence rubs off on me, so I add, 'That's right, thank you.'

Then it hits me. This is Harrods. Arabella is a personal shopper. There's no way I can possibly afford this. Lucas must pick up on my flash of worry because he leans closer and whispers in my ear, 'It's my gift.'

Shaking my head, I meet his eyes. 'No. You can't.'

'Yes. I can.' He presses his lips to my cheek. 'Give us a moment, would you, Arabella?'

'Of course. Shall I pull some outfits together in the meantime?' she asks.

'That would be great.' Lucas nods and she sashays away. 'Carla, do you think I'd bring you here to purchase a party outfit and not pay for it? I'm not a monster.'

'I know that.' My laughter is tinged with anxiety. 'But I don't want to be your charity case.'

'Look ...' A small line appears between his brows and deepens as he inhales slowly. 'This is my gift to thank you for coming to the party with me and for all the fantastic meals you've made me this week. I don't see you as a charity case, nor do I pity you. I really like you, Carla, and I have plenty of money, so please let me spend some of it on you. For old times' sake and for the fantastic time we're having together now.'

Chewing at my lower lip, I think about what he's said, but it's so hard. He's already letting me stay with him for free and now he wants to pay for clothes for me. I do have some pride, but I also know that when someone wants to offer you a gift, it's rude to decline because it can hurt their feelings.

'Let me spoil you, Carla. I don't have anyone else to spoil.'

His eyes are filled with sincerity, and it makes my stomach do a loop the loop. How can he be so kind, handsome and sexy? This very rich man wants to spoil me. What are the chances of that happening?

'Lucas ... this is difficult for me.'

'I know. Look ... How about if we agree that when you're settled, I'll come and stay with you as your guest and you can spoil me then? How does that sound?'

So this wouldn't be the end? I'd see more of him? I almost kick my heels together there and then.

'That sounds fair.' I smile and move to my tiptoes and press a kiss to his cheek, but he turns and pulls me against him then kisses me hard on the mouth, taking my breath away.

'Then that's a deal.' He waggles his eyebrows at me. 'Now let's get you undressed.'

'What?'

'So you can try on some outfits.' The glint in his eyes tells me he was only half joking.

I let him lead me to the changing rooms, all the while wondering if he intends to undress me himself.

Chapter 25

Lucas

I sit back on the plush velvet sofa and sip the champagne Arabella offered me. Carla goes behind a plush red velvet curtain and tries on the dresses Arabella brought for her on a rail. There's a range of colours and styles and I'm looking forward to seeing her wearing them. I was tempted to help Carla undress, and it was only Arabella's presence that stopped me. I knew that seeing Carla in her lingerie would make me hard, and then I'd struggle to keep my hands to myself. Since I already have plans for later, I should probably hold back from instructing Arabella to give us some alone time. Nevertheless, my cock twitches in my trousers, teasing me with thoughts of what I want to ask Carla later. This will be a Christmas party like no other, that's for sure...

The next thirty minutes are delicious torture as Carla emerges in dress after dress, displaying her gorgeous curves and sometimes more flesh than I'd want anyone else to see. I'm surprised by my feelings of jealousy and possessiveness when I picture another man seeing her in revealing attire.

Starting Over With the Billionaire

She's not mine and yet I feel proprietorial about her, especially when it comes to other men who might want to ogle her or even do more. My free hand clenches into a fist at the thought and I grind my teeth together. No man better go near her this evening, and I think I have one way to ensure that she's off limits. Not that I think she would entertain another man when I'm around, but I've had an idea and since it occurred to me, I can't get it out of my head.

We've yet to fuck fully, but when we do, I don't want anything between us. I want to feel every part of Carla around every part of me, her sweet cunt dripping over my cock the way it drips over my fingers and tongue.

Man, I can't wait for later...

Chapter 26

Carla

I am dizzy by the time we have decided on a dress, shoes, bag, and jewellery and exhausted by the effort of not checking the prices on everything. The first dress had a tag on it that made my eyes water and so I tried not to look again after that. What's the point? Lucas won't allow me to refuse his generosity and so I decided to fully embrace it.

When Arabella mentions lingerie, I nod like I have another woman pick out my underwear all the time, and then I take a moment to sit with Lucas in the changing room lounge.

'Here.' He hands me a glass of champagne and I take a grateful sip.

'Thanks.' The champagne is crisp and light and the alcohol hits my stomach and warms it, spreading out to the rest of my body and soothing any remaining anxiety.

'Are you having fun?' His blue eyes sparkle as he smiles at me and it's all I can do not to wrap my arms around him and tell him I want to be this way forever.

'I am. And it's all thanks to you. Again.' Raising the glass, I take a gulp because for some reason I suddenly feel like I might cry.

'Hey, what's wrong?'

'Nothing. I ...' Blinking hard, I sip more of the drink, hoping it will soothe me.

'You what?' The concern etched on his features makes me even more emotional, and I close my eyes so I don't have to gaze at his handsome face any longer. 'Have I said or done something?'

He cups my cheek with his right hand, and I open my eyes, but his image is blurry.

'No. Y-you've done everything ... perfectly. It's just that all this is ...'

'Upsetting you?' He leans closer and takes my face in both his hands now, holds my gaze.

'Not this. Y-you. No ... not you. Just ... I'm overwhelmed. This is all so incredible and being here with you at this time of year is amazing. I'm just very grateful that I don't have to be alone at Christmas.'

'Oh, Carla, love ...' He kisses me softly on the lips, then kisses away my tears and something in my chest shifts, then cracks wide open, and I sag against him. 'I'm glad you're with me, too. We'll have a Christmas to remember.' He kisses me again and I melt against his mouth, moan softly as his tongue tangles with mine and his hands move down my throat and rest on my collar bones then move around to my back and he pulls me closer to him. My skin tingles all over and heat ignites at my core in the places he has touched me, the places that remember him and want more of him.

All of him.

Every single inch of that gorgeous cock of his, so I can feel him filling me up, making me whole again.

'I need you,' I whisper, opening my eyes. I gaze into the depths of his blue eyes that make me think of tropical pools and rainstorms, of summer days and happy times, of sex and orgasms and afternoon naps. Lucas could so easily become everything to me and that is something I cannot allow because for him, this is only temporary and, I must remind myself, for me too. I was widowed not even a year ago and so I need to keep my walls built up around me. It's just so hard when this man touches me, kisses me and holds me close. Men like Lucas are made for falling in love with over and over again.

'OK then.' Arabella is back and so I reluctantly let go of Lucas and stand up, drain the glass of champagne, then go to see what she has for me. As she holds up the different items made of silk and lace, I glance back at Lucas and find him watching us, something in his eyes that's not quite lust and not quite love.

What is it then that's going on inside his head and heart? I wish I knew, but suspect it's better that I don't.

Chapter 27

Lucas

Back at my apartment, I place the bags on Carla's bed while she hangs the dress she chose for this evening on the front of the wardrobe.

'Thank you again for all this,' she says, gazing at the bags. 'I can't believe you bought it all for me.'

'It's a pleasure.'

After we'd purchased the clothes, we went to the salon in Harrods, and she had her hair and makeup done. I sat and waited in the adjacent chair, conducting some business on my phone and watching as the stylist pampered Carla. She seems so new to all of this, and it tugs at my heart. It's like she's never been spoilt before and that hurts me; a woman as lovely as she is should always be made to feel special. At least now, I can do these things for her and show her how amazing I think she is, even it's just temporary. As far as the money is concerned, it's not like I don't have plenty of it and then some. I mean, I have my apartment and monthly outgoings, but it's nothing I can't manage and spending on

Carla is a pleasure. She doesn't seem to want a penny of my money, and that makes it even more enjoyable. Carla has no expectations of me, and I like that. Some of the women I've dated in the past have wanted things from me, so I've quickly sent them packing, but Carla is easygoing and happy to simply be with me. It's refreshing. Carla is refreshing. She is, quite simply put, an original. How some bastard could have hurt her and made her feel like she had no value is beyond me. I hope he realises what he lost one day and regrets it big time. I also hope she never entertains the thought of giving him a second chance because men like that don't deserve women like Carla in their lives.

Carla admires her hair in the mirror. It's been styled in curls, then pinned in a messy up do with tendrils caressing her cheeks and nape. It's incredibly sexy and I've been longing to kiss her neck since we left the salon. The makeup artist did her makeup for an evening reception, giving her a flawless complexion and smoky eyes. She darkened her long, fair lashes with mascara and curled them to frame her pretty grey eyes. She looks incredible.

'Would you like a drink?' I ask.

'What're you thinking?'

'We started with champagne, so I thought we might as well continue.'

'Sounds good to me.' She tugs her bottom lip between her teeth and my dick jumps to attention.

In the kitchen, I get a bottle from the wine fridge, then pop the cork and fill two flutes. Carla joins me wearing the fluffy purple robe we picked up in Harrods. It's soft and warm and I hope she'll get lots of wear out of it when she leaves. Perhaps she'll remember me when she wears it.

We move to the lounge and sit close to each other on the sofa.

'Here's to a wonderful evening where you'll meet my friends and stun them with your beauty,' I say. At least with Edward and Jack being married, I know I don't have to worry about them around Carla. Not that I don't trust them, but men are men and I don't like the thought of anyone looking at Carla in a lustful way. No one but me, that is.

I sip my champagne then set my glass on the table.

'Carla ... I had a thought and I want to know how you feel about it.'

She sips her drink, then places her flute next to mine on the table.

'OK.'

Meeting her pretty grey eyes, I drink her in. 'I want to make love to you properly. I've been holding back because I didn't want to rush. Also, I know you've been hurt in the past and I have my own ... demons, but I've been enjoying our time together immensely. However.... I can't deny that the thought of being inside you turns me on so fucking bad.'

'Me too,' she breathes, then licks her full lips.

'But I hate the thought of anything being in the way.'

'What do you mean?' She frowns then rubs a hand over her chest and I have to hold myself back from pushing open the robe to see if she's wearing anything underneath it.

'I mean ...' I inhale sharply. 'That I want to feel you without a barrier ... without a condom.'

'Oh ...' Her brows raise.

'Does that shock you?'

'A ... a bit, I guess. But I know what you mean.' Her cheeks flush and I hope I haven't worried her.

'I've been tested. I have regular tests as part of my private health care, and I never have unprotected sex. But even so, I'm tested for everything regularly. I can show you the latest documentation if you'd like.'

She shakes her head. 'It's OK. I trust you.'

'I'm glad to hear that.' I smile.

'I'm clear too,' she blurts. 'I–I had to have tests done after ... well ... earlier this year. For my peace of mind.'

'Did something happen?' I take her hand and stroke the back of it, run my finger up each of hers in turn. The skin is so soft. I notice that she's removed the wedding ring and my heart gives a little jump.

'I wanted to know that I was OK. Kind of a reflex I guess, after what happened.'

Nodding slowly, I sigh. That bastard must have really worried Carla and put her health in jeopardy, and that's something I'd never do.

'I can show you my test results if you like?' she offers and I swear my heart breaks a little.

'I trust you too, Carla. It's not like we're strangers in a bar who've just met. We have history.'

'We do, and you know what?'

I shake my head.

'I find it comforting that we do. We've known each other for a long time and it's nice. This thing between us is ... ummm ... it's natural and it's ... *organic*.' She laughs as she finds the word she was looking for.

'I agree.' Raising her hand, I press a kiss to the palm.

'So you want to make love to me without ... anything between us?' she asks.

'There's one more issue though.'

'I have the contraceptive implant.'

'So ...' I smile. 'We're good to go. When we feel ready, that is.'

'We are.'

Our eyes meet and I take her pretty face in my hands and lean towards her then kiss her softly. She has never looked more beautiful to me than she does right now. I pull her onto my lap and hold her against my chest. Now I know we can make love the way I want, I'm in no rush. Being with her like this, holding her, is enough. We have two weeks left together so we can take our time and when we're both ready, we can explore each other like never before.

Chapter 28

Carla

I had a fabulous day. After Lucas had spoilt me at Harrods, I had my hair and makeup done in the salon there, as well as my nails, and I now feel like a princess. Standing in front of the mirror in my room, I move from side to side, watching as the new dress hugs my curves. I can hardly believe it's me because I look so different. It's amazing what money and pampering can do.

What would Kofi think if he could see me now? Would he like this version of me or would it hurt him to see me like this because he could never provide this for me, nor could I for him? I never cared for money or things during our time together because our love was all I wanted, but now he's gone, I guess I can enjoy this and what Lucas can offer me for a short period of time.

I head into the ensuite and pick up my perfume, then spray it in the air and walk into the fine mist. It envelops me and I turn, then repeat the action. A heady combination of pomegranate and pink pepper uplifts me and I smile at my reflection above the sink.

Back in the bedroom, I pick up my velvet wrap and bag, then take a deep breath and leave the room. I hope Lucas will like what he sees. Right now, his approval matters more than anything.

Chapter 29

Lucas

I'm adjusting the cuffs of my shirt when Carla emerges from the bedroom and I swear my jaw drops. She is stunning in the green silk dress with lace sleeves and a revealing bodice that accentuates her large breasts, while the floaty skirt drifts around her ankles. The dark green suits her colouring and I am suddenly ravenous, but not for food.

I am ravenous for this woman who is everything a woman should be and more. She is a vision and I want her.

Now.

No more waiting.

I cross the room in a few strides and take her arms, pull her against me, then lower my head and kiss her. She gasps against my lips and while still kissing her; I take the wrap and bag from her hands and throw them onto the sofa, then press my hand against the front of the dress over her breasts. She moans so I reach down and find the hem of the dress then lift it and slip my hand between her thighs. My palm brushes against lace so I push it aside and touch her soaking wet pussy, slide my fingers between those slick lower lips. I find her swollen clit, then rub two fingers on either side of it before plunging them deep inside her.

'Carla.' My voice is deeper than usual, thick with desire. 'It has to be now.'

'No more waiting?' she asks.

'No more waiting.' I pick her up and carry her to the sofa, then set her down next to it before turning her around. 'Put your hands on the arm.'

She bends over and holds the arm of the sofa and I lift that pretty dress again and expose her curvy bottom. Tugging the thong over it and down her thighs, I let it slip to her ankles then she kicks her feet out of it. The green heels she's wearing make her tilt her ass forwards even more at the perfect angle. I rub my hands over her cheeks and my cock strains against my trousers so I unzip them and reach inside, pull my erection free.

Carla's pussy glistens in the lamplight, inviting me inside, and so I run my cock over the entrance to her body, my pre-cum mixing with her juices. When I ease the tip inside her, she whimpers.

'Breathe slowly, love. You can take it. All of it.'

She breathes in and I inch my cock into her, slowly, moving it from side to side to stretch her. The pink skin of her pussy stretches around my girth, and it feels so good I could blow my load right now. But I don't. *The lady comes first* is a rule I live by.

When I am buried to the hilt inside Carla, I hold her left hip tight, then reach my right hand around and caress her hard clit, feeling it swell even more under my touch. I pump into her, slowly at first as I savour the feel of her cunt clenching around me and then faster and faster as my excitement builds.

'Lucas ... I'm coming!' She pushes against me as she explodes, squirting all over my cock and balls, and I slow down to let her enjoy every spasm. When she is done, I speed up again, driving my cock into her, skin against skin, heat against heat. I fuck her hard, feeling her bumping against the arm of the sofa as my cock bumps against her core, my fingers digging into the flesh of her hips as her ass ripples beneath my touch.

As I erupt into her, I roar, my cock jerking again and again as it empties into her body, filling her with my seed.

Leaning over her, I hold her body against me while our breathing slows before I ease out of her. My cock is wet with her juices and my cum. It pleases me knowing that I've left part of myself inside her.

I turn her and lift her onto the arm of the sofa then push her backwards so I can get a proper look at her pussy.

'So wet, love.' I smile my approval then touch a finger to her entrance, push my seed back into her. 'Keep that inside you this evening so you can remember how well I fucked you.'

She looks up at me, excitement in her gaze, so I rub my thumb over her clit and she throws her head back, shivers as a thrill runs through her.

Starting Over With the Billionaire

'When we get home, I'll be back inside this beautiful pussy for more.'

'I can't wait,' she says with a smile.

I tidy myself up, then help her step into her thong. As I slide it up her thighs, I lean forward and kiss her pussy, suck hard at her clit and she grabs my head with both hands.

'I'm sensitive.' She pulls my head against her so all I can smell and taste is pussy. Well, if the lady wants more right now, then that's what she's going to get.

I lick and suck at her clit while I grip her ass hard and it's seconds before she comes again, this time all over my face. I keep eating her until her shuddering ends, then I pull her thong up and lower her dress.

'You're the sexiest woman I've ever had the pleasure of fucking.' I kiss her mouth and push my tongue inside her so she can taste what I can. 'I could eat you all day long, then hammer my cock into you until we both come again.'

'Later.' Her grey eyes are filled with mischief.

'Later,' I agree.

But as we head to our bathrooms to wash up before we leave, I know that later can't come soon enough.

Chapter 30

Carla

The journey from London to Buckinghamshire takes about an hour and a half. I sit back in the limo and gaze at the scenery as it rushes past. Dark shapes and shadows of the countryside give way to festive lights and decorations on roofs and in windows. It is snowing again but slowly; the flakes glowing in the headlights as they fall to the road. Lucas sits at my side, holding my hand, tracing circles on the palm and it relaxes me, helps me to feel less anxious about meeting his friends.

The limo comes to a stop outside ornate, wrought-iron gates that swing inwards, then we travel along a winding driveway, tall snow topped trees towering either side of us. Now and then we pass houses that Lucas tells me belong to some of the Cavendish estate employees and one that Edward's mother-in-law lives in with her young son.

The limo stops in front of a large stately home, its red brick exterior illuminated by low lights positioned behind planters in front of the building. A quick count reveals three storeys and seven bays wide, as well as a parapet and attic windows. Even though it's dark, I can make out large lawns bordering the driveway that stretch away for as far as I can see, snow covering them like a pure, cold blanket. This is a house bought with a lot of money, I think, and this is how other people live. I could never afford a house like this but for me, there are far more important things than money. Money can't buy your life back, and losing my husband as I did, means I know that health is the most important gift of all. That and love.

'I promise you that Edward and Ava are not at all stuck up or snobby,' Lucas says as the driver opens the door and we get out. I pull my wrap tighter around me because it's chilly, and the wind seems to rush across the gardens, fresh and bracing.

Lucas takes my arm and leads me up the steps to the front door, where a member of the household waits to let us inside.

No sooner have we entered the house than a handsome man and a beautiful woman greet us, and I know instantly that this is Edward and Ava. He is tall with thick dark hair, a beard, and dark brown eyes, and she has amber eyes and shiny brown hair pulled into a high ponytail. She's about my height, although as we're both wearing heels it's hard to tell exactly. They are holding hands and both smiling warmly at us, and I feel suddenly shy.

'Lucas!' Edward embraces his friend, then turns to me. 'And this must be Carla. Hello and welcome. I'm Edward and this is my wife, Ava.'

'Yes, welcome to our home.' Ava kisses me on both cheeks then Edward does the same. I try not to stare at my surroundings because the house is seriously impressive. 'I love your dress, Carla!'

'Thanks.' I smile. 'I love yours too.'

As I admire the red bodycon dress, I notice her tummy is rounded and when I look up again, she's grinning. She places a hand over the slight bump and nods. 'I'm pregnant.'

'Congratulations!'

'Thanks. We're delighted although not as delighted as Joe, who can't wait for his baby brother to arrive.'

'It's a boy then?' Lucas asks as he slides his arm around my waist.

Ava meets her husband's eyes, and a secret smile passes between them.

'We don't know yet, truth be told,' Edward says, 'but that's what Joe has his heart set on. I guess we'll have to wait and see.'

The door behind us opens as more guests arrive, and Edward looks over my shoulder and waves.

'We'll get a drink and catchup in a bit,' Lucas says, and he leads me away.

'You didn't tell me that Ava was pregnant.' I smile as we pass some people.

'Didn't I?' Lucas shrugs. 'Sorry, it must have slipped my mind.'

'It's quite an important detail. I could have said something rude to her.' The thought makes me shudder because the last thing I want is to upset Lucas' friends.

'Like what?' He stops me and peers into my face.

'Well ... Like... I could have asked if she was pregnant but she was just a bit bloated.'

Lucas laughs. 'Don't be silly. No one gets that bloated.'

'You'd be surprised. You haven't seen me if I eat too much wheat.'

'You'd be gorgeous bloated or not. I love your body.'

He takes my arm, and we walk through the hallway and enter a doorway on the left. There's a bar in the corner and as we approach it, Lucas says, 'Probably best if I let you know Grace is pregnant, too.'

'Jack's wife?'

He nods.

'Anything else I should know now before I meet more of your friends?'

'I don't think so.'

At the bar, he orders champagne and when we have our glasses, we cross the room and stand before a large fireplace.

'I think I probably didn't tell you about the pregnancies because things like that don't tend to occur to me as important,' he says. 'It's just people getting on with their lives and lots of my friends have children now. We're at that age where settling down and breeding seems like the next step for some.'

'But not for you?' I gaze at him in his black tuxedo, the jacket cut so perfectly for him I know it must be custom made.

His brows meet above his straight nose, and he rubs at his neck. 'Not for me, no. I just ... I don't think I'd be a good parent.'

'Why not?' Sipping my drink, I observe his reaction to the question. A range of emotions cross his handsome features as he thinks about how to answer me.

'My ummm ... My childhood wasn't the best.'

Tilting my head, I reach for his hand. 'I didn't know that.'

He sighs and stares at his shiny shoes. 'Few do. It's not something I like to shout from the rooftops. Nobody likes a whinger, right?' He laughs, but I know him well enough to understand that this is a front, a façade he adopts to hide what's going on inside. I don't know him well enough to know exactly what he's thinking or feeling, but I'm getting better at reading him.

'Lucas, the last thing you are is a whinger.'

'Yeah but it's easy to fall into that trap. I'd rather be busy and productive than sitting around feeling sorry for myself.'

'I know.' Nodding, I sip my drink. He does keep busy, whether it's working at the office or at home, working out or having sex with me. He barely seems to sleep, is always up early and rushing around, and even when we chill together, I sense restlessness inside him. Constant momentum must be how he avoids dwelling on the things that have hurt him. 'But it is OK to talk about your feelings and the things that have made you who you are today.'

'Maybe.' He looks across the room and I see something change in his face, like he's shutting me out. Have I pushed too far? 'But I do know that the whole marriage and babies thing isn't for me.' He meets my gaze, his blue eyes cold as a frozen lake, and a shiver runs down my spine. Is this how he's stayed single then? By shutting all feelings down the minute he's reminded of his past?

'You're entitled to live your life your way,' I say, then I down my champagne and hold up my glass. 'Shall we get another?'

'Sure.' He takes my glass and we wander over to the bar, this time not holding hands, and I feel a distance between us that wasn't there before. Have I reminded him of his resolve not to care for anyone then? It saddens me that he can react this way, but I can also understand it. When you've been hurt, whatever form that pain came in, it's easier to shut down and stop feeling than it is to deal with everything openly. It just makes me feel bad for Lucas because he's a wonderful human being with so much to offer to the right person. Maybe he hasn't found that person yet, but when he does, everything will change for him and hopefully he'll be able to move on from his past.

The rest of the evening is thoroughly enjoyable as Lucas introduces me to friends and colleagues and I get to speak to Ava again and to meet Grace. At one point, Lucas excuses himself, leaving me with Ava and Grace in the beautiful library. I could spend some serious time in this room, just sniffing the amazing scent of books and losing myself between the pages.

'Have a seat.' Ava gestures at a chaise longue near the French doors and I sit and cross my ankles.

Ava and Grace sit on a damask velvet sofa opposite and for a moment I feel like I'm about to be interviewed. Outside the French doors, the snow swirls down, heavier now than when we arrived. On the terrace, four Christmas trees stand in stone planters, their colourful lights swaying in the chilly breeze. It's a perfect festive scene.

I turn my head and look over at Ava and Grace. The latter is clearly pregnant and her bump looks bigger than Ava's. She's a beautiful woman too, with long, wavy blonde hair, and emerald eyes framed by long lashes. Her black dress has a square neckline and a ruched waist that is stretched over the swell of her belly, and my eyes are drawn to it as I wonder how far along she is. The skirt falls to her ankles, and she's wearing flat black pumps, not the heels most women here this evening are wearing.

'I currently have cankles,' she says.

'Sorry?'

'Cankles. The pregnancy has made my ankles swell up so there's no difference between my calves and my ankles.'

'Oh ...' I smile because I don't know how to respond.

'You do not have cankles.' Ava places a hand on Grace's arm. 'Just a touch of oedema, but it's normal when you're carrying twins.'

Grace places both hands on her belly and nods. 'Twins. I can still barely believe it.'

'Congratulations!' I say, impressed to think that she has not one but two babies in her belly.

'I'm not even as far along as Ava as I'm only just five months pregnant, but I'm already bigger than her because I'm carrying two babies. And you've seen Jack. He's not exactly small so I'm a bit worried about how big these babies are going to get.'

'Do you know what you're having?' I ask.

Grace grins at me. 'I do. We're having boys!'

'Oh my goodness, that's amazing!' I clap my hands, excited for her.

'Jack is over the moon and can't wait to be a dad.' Her eyes glisten and she opens her bag and pulls out a tissue. 'Here come the waterworks again.'

'Pregnancy is a tough time emotionally.' Ava rubs her friend's back.

'Do you have any children?' Grace asks me, then her eyes widen. 'I'm so sorry ... I never know if I'm supposed to ask that these days. Some things are now considered inappropriate for conversation, aren't they?'

'I think it's OK to ask if someone has a family,' Ava says.

'It's fine, honestly,' I reply. 'And the answer is no, I don't have any children and I've never been pregnant. I did want to start a family in the next few years, but ... well ... things didn't work out that way.' I sip my drink and look out of the doors across the lawns. Life works out for some and not for others, although everyone has their challenges. It's nice to sit here with these two women and to see them so happy with their lives and their partners, pregnancy hormones aside.

'I hope you're OK now?' Grace asks and I nod.

'I'm OK. What can we do other than keep going through whatever life throws at us?'

'That's true.' Ava nods now. 'How are things going with Lucas? If you don't mind me asking.'

'Oh ... we're friends.' I shift my position on the chaise and nibble at a cuticle.

'Friends?' She frowns. 'I thought you were staying with him?'

'I am. But we, uh ... know each other from childhood. He was my brother's best friend growing up, and he spent a lot of time at our home. As adults, though ... we've got a lot ... closer.'

Stop talking, Carla!

The women watch me expectantly, clearly waiting for me to elaborate.

'We're ... I guess... friends with benefits.' I give a small laugh to break the tension and I see Ava's lips twitch.

'Is that what it is?' she says.

'I think so.' I bite the inside of my cheek, wishing I could think of a reason to leave the library that wouldn't seem rude.

'Edward said he's seen a difference in Lucas since you arrived.' Ava stares at me, mischief in her eyes. 'He said he seems a lot happier than usual.'

'That's nice.'

Eeek!

'Jack said the same,' Grace adds. 'It's like Lucas has changed. He's always been a good man, but he can be such a joker and seem quite hard if you don't know him very well. But since you arrived, he's definitely warmer and less of a prankster.'

'Oh ...' I blink at the two women and wonder if hormones make people this blunt and nosey.

'I'm sorry, you must feel like we're prying,' Ava says then. 'We don't mean to, but we're a close bunch and we care about Lucas and would love to see him settle down. You seem to be good for him and that's such a positive thing for us all to see. You're certainly good for him, whatever you're doing.'

Heat seeps into my cheeks, and I smile. They think I'm good for Lucas and that I'm making him happier, and it's nice to hear.

'Thank you.' I smile, then stand up. 'If you can excuse me, I need to use the bathroom?'

'Of course.' Avan stands and is about to walk me to the door, but I shake my head.

'I can find it. You rest. I'm sure it's hard carrying a baby around all day.'

She giggles and rubs her belly. 'Oh my goodness, it's so tiring. I could sleep for England. But it's also exciting knowing that next Christmas we'll have a new addition to celebrate with us.'

'That's very exciting.' I smile warmly at Ava and Grace, then leave the library and wander out into the hallway, looking for the most likely direction of the nearest toilet. As I stand there, I feel something trickle out of my sex and I gasp. 'No!' Lucas' cum is oozing out of me and I don't think my lace thong will be much of a barrier to it for long.

'Hey!'

I turn and see Lucas standing in the hallway — tall, dark and handsome.

My lover!

My heart leaps.

'Hey yourself,' I say flirtatiously, keen to leave the serious tone we shared earlier behind.

'Where are you going?' he asks.

'I need to find a bathroom,' I reply, pressing my thighs together to stop his cum leaking down my legs.

'Why are you standing like that? Are you bursting?' he laughs as he approaches me.

'I don't actually need the toilet. It's your ... cum,' I whisper. 'It's about to trickle down my thighs.'

'I see.' His eyes darken as he takes hold of my arms and kisses me. His lips are so warm and soft and he smells so good that I lean into him, forgetting that we're standing in the hallway of his friend's mansion. 'Come here.' He leans over, tucks his arm beneath my legs and lifts me against his chest.

'Lucas! What if someone sees?'

'I'll say you twisted your ankle and I'm taking you to the bathroom to administer first aid.'

With that, he returns the way he came and carries me up the wide staircase and across the landing, then pushes open a door and carries me inside.

He sets me down and turns on the light then locks the door. I look around the large bathroom with a clawfoot tub, double shower enclosure, and sash windows overlooking the gardens. Everything is white, from the bath to the tiles to the rugs on the floor. It's pristine and smells of lemon and basil, fresh and herby. Lucas comes to me and kisses me again, holding my chin in his large right hand while the other cups my bottom.

When he moves back and meets my gaze, he's grinning. 'Now let's sort out your issue, shall we?'

He bends down and takes hold of my dress, then lifts it slowly up my legs. The material whispers against my skin and goosebumps rise all over me. 'Hold your dress above your waist.'

'What?' I giggle.

'Do it.' The command in his voice sends heat to my core, so I take hold of the dress and do as he told me. Looking across the room, I meet my eyes in the mirror and see a woman I barely recognise. My eyes are dark, my cheeks rosy and I look wanton, not gaunt and sad as I have grown used to seeing for so long. 'Let's get this thong off.'

Lucas takes hold of the thong and peels it down my thighs, growling as he exposes my sex. When it reaches my ankles, he raises them one at a time to loop the lace garment over my feet.

When he kisses my sex, I shiver with pleasure.

'You smell so hot right now,' he says, 'The perfect combination of you and me.'

He takes hold of my bottom and pulls me towards him, then he nestles his mouth between my lips and starts to hum. The vibrations tickle and arouse me and soon I'm wobbling on my heels, but he holds me tight, so tight I suspect his fingertips will leave bruises on my skin. The humming continues relentlessly, tickling, teasing, rousing.

I'm pinned against him.

I can't move.

And soon I feel my orgasm tingling at my core then radiating through my sex and outwards until I shudder violently against him and cry out his name.

When he pulls back and peers up at me, his mouth is wet with our combined juices. His eyes are filled with hunger. Hunger for me. This man wants me just as I want him.

I pull away from him and go to the freestanding bathtub, then bend over it. I grip the edge of the bathtub with my right hand while my left keeps my dress up high. Lucas can get an excellent view of my dripping wet sex from here and his feral growl tells me he's enjoying it.

When his hands grip my hips and he pushes my legs further apart with a knee, I know I'm in for a treat.

I hear his zip being lowered and then feel his erection pressing between my cheeks before he slides it lower and penetrates me. He's so big and so hard that I pulse around him, excited by how incredible it feels when he fills me and stretches me like this. He glides in and out of me and the tip of his cock hits my G-spot and I ride the waves of pleasure once again.

Starting Over With the Billionaire

'What do you want, Carla?' he asks, his voice dark with desire.

'I want you to fuck me,' I say, panting with the effort of staying upright.

He takes my hands from the side of the bath and turns me away from it without withdrawing from my body, then pushes me over and places both my hands around my ankles. I thank myself for the years of doing yoga several times a week, which means this isn't uncomfortable. Lucas starts to pump again and the angle means that he's hitting my G-pot perfectly, as well as my cervix. It's a kind of painful pleasure that excites me and an orgasm ricochets through me, taking me by surprise. Lucas keeps pumping, faster and harder and I feel him swelling, the veins in his cock pulsing, so when he stops, I think he's about to come. Instead, he pulls out of me and takes my shoulders so I'm standing upright. He steadies me for a moment and I'm glad as it gives me a headrush, then he turns me to face him and kisses my lips. I drink him in, still fully dressed in his tux but with his giant cock poking out of his trousers, soaked in our combined fluids.

'Now this way.' He scoops me off my feet and lays me down on the rug. He kneels between my legs then pulls my hips onto his lap and rests my heels on his shoulders as he enters me. While he grinds into me, he holds me in position with one hand and the other moves between my legs and circles my clit. It's sensitive from today's orgasms but he knows how to turn me on and he rubs me in such a way that I'm soon aroused. We soon come together, eyes locked, his cock pulsing into me until I am once more filled with his seed.

When he releases me, he helps me to my feet and kisses me.

'Are you OK?' he asks. 'I didn't mean to be quite so demanding then, but I couldn't help myself.'

'I'm more than OK,' I say.

'Let's get you cleaned up and we'd better return to the party.'

'We probably should.' I laugh as he leads me to the sink, because I still have my dress held up around my waist and his semi-hard cock is still poking out of his fly.

But I know it's OK to be like this with him. We have something that means we can screw hard, then laugh together. We are not just lovers; we are friends, and as I said to Ava and Grace, we are friends with benefits.

And as Lucas tenderly cleans me up, then helps me step into my thong, I know he is healing me, one fuck at a time. One tender act at a time. One day at a time.

I have no idea how I'm going to walk away from him when the time comes, but I do know that he's not offering me the option to stay. He has his own demons and I have to understand.

Difficult as it is to accept that, the time will come when I will need to let him go.

Chapter 31

Carla

Two days after the party, Lucas comes to my room early and tells me to stay in bed and rest because he has to pop out for something. I'm tired and it's cold outside of the covers, so I don't argue at all. The bed is more comfortable than any bed I've ever slept on and so I curl up and close my eyes again, relaxing as sleep reclaims me.

When I wake, my phone tells me it's after nine and I can hear noises from the lounge. I contemplate staying where I am, but curiosity forces me to rise and I use the bathroom then put on my fluffy robe and head to the lounge.

'Oh my goodness!' I exclaim as I see what Lucas has been up to.

'Surprise!' He holds out his arms and gestures to the area in front of the windows that he's cleared to make space for a tree. 'What do you think?'

I shake my head, smiling. 'It's lovely.'

'I bought some decorations for it and some lights, so I thought we could decorate it together.'

'That's so sweet of you.' This is not the Lucas I used to know, nor is it the hard-headed businessman I expected. This is a completely different Lucas, and it proves to me that we all have different sides to us.

'I also bought breakfast so shall we eat first then get decorating?'

He goes to the kitchen island and picks up a brown paper bag and two disposable coffee cups and takes them to the lounge, then sets them on the table. I sit in the corner of the sofa and curl my legs up underneath me. The smell of pine is strong, and it takes me back to the festive seasons of my childhood. A flicker of something I haven't felt in an age stirs in my stomach and I place a hand there for a moment as if to hold on to it.

'You OK?' Lucas asks, his eyes filled with concern.

'I felt something then.' Meeting his eyes, I add, 'I think it was a throwback to childhood.'

'Something good?' His eyebrows ascend leisurely, and I nod.

'I think it was excitement. I haven't felt it in a very long time.'

'Oh ...' He chews at his bottom lip. 'I thought I'd excited you more than once since you came to stay.'

His comment makes me laugh. 'Not that type of excitement. I meant the kind that you get as a child when you're looking forward to something.'

Starting Over With the Billionaire

'Like Christmas?'

'Don't you remember that feeling? The awareness that on Christmas Eve, Father Christmas will come to your home with the gifts you asked for and you'll spend time with family and friends and eat nice food. If you're really lucky, you'll get some snow.'

Lucas' eyes change and he looks away, then rubs a hand over his brow.

'What is it?' I shuffle over on the sofa and touch his arm.

He shakes his head then reaches for the coffees and hands me one. 'Not every child has magical Christmases, Carla.'

'Lucas, I know that.' Unease fills me. 'I didn't mean that they do but ... I did and I thought you would have done too.'

'My, um ... my childhood wasn't all that perfect.' He sighs, then seems to shake himself. 'But it doesn't matter right now. This matters. Us here. Together.' He meets my gaze, and his eyes are bright blue again as if a cloud passed over them and now the sun has emerged again.

'Lucas ... you can trust me. Tell me, please.'

Silence falls between us and my left thumb goes to rub my wedding ring in a comfort gesture, but it's not there. I feel shock for a moment, but it fades as I remember that I've stopped wearing it. Taking it off after so long wasn't easy, but it didn't seem right to continue wearing it when I'm having sex with another man. I've tucked it away safely in my purse. I don't know if I'll wear it again when I leave here. Perhaps I will and perhaps I won't. What I know is that whether or not I'm wearing his ring, Kofi will always be in my heart.

Lucas takes a sip of his coffee, then smiles at me. 'It's fine. Nothing to tell.'

I consider trying to press him to explain, but I don't want to ruin the moment and so I don't. If he wanted to tell me, he would.

'OK then.' Hurt prickles through me, but I can also understand. Sometimes we don't want to talk about the things that hurt us. All the advice these days is that sharing helps, and bottling things up isn't good for us, but sometimes telling someone means we have to go through the pain again. It can be easier to push it all aside and wait for another time. A time that may never come.

'Here.' He opens the brown bag and pulls out a bacon and cheese croissant wrapped in a paper serviette. 'These are delicious.'

Accepting the croissant, I take a bite and the buttery goodness fills my mouth. The pastry is light and flaky, the bacon is crisp and salty and the cheese is creamy in contrast. Without even trying, I take bite after bite until I'm sucking my fingers clean, then wiping them with the serviette.

When I look up, Lucas is watching me, his mouth open, his eyes dark.

'What?' I lick a crumb of pastry from the corner of my mouth, and he pounces like a wild animal. Covering me with his body, he squashes me into the corner of the sofa. 'Lucas!' I giggle, but I'm also a tiny bit scared at how strong he is.

'Fuck, Carla, watching you eat that was the hottest thing I've ever seen.' He tugs my legs from under me and spreads them, then pulls the belt of my robe and opens it. I reach for him but he takes my hands and puts them above my head, then he strokes down my neck and my chest, his fingers tracing over my nipples through the thin satin of my nightdress. He reaches lower and lifts the hem, then feels beneath it and groans. 'No panties.'

He unbuttons his jeans and without even pulling them down, he's pressing that giant cock against me and soon it's inside me. He takes me fast and furious on the sofa and we both come quickly, skin against skin, the taste of his croissant on his lips as he kisses me passionately enough to steal my breath.

'I'm sorry,' he says. 'I should have made that last longer.'

'Don't be sorry. It was gorgeous.'

'Are you sure? I never want to let you down.'

'Lucas, a quickie is just right sometimes.'

'Yeah ... That's what I thought.' He winks then slides out of me and adjusts his jeans before gently pulling my nightdress down and closing my robe. When I hold out my hands, he pulls me up and gives me my coffee. 'Not even cold.'

'That's impressive.' We laugh then drink our coffee, sitting side by side on his sofa, gazing at the tree.

An hour later, we've decorated the tree with the lights and some of the silver baubles Lucas bought and then he holds out a box the size of a shoebox.

'What's this?' I ask.

Wynter Wilde

'Open it.'

'I hope it's not trainers for me to start running.' I laugh, but I'm only half joking. Running has never really appealed to me. Kofi used to run all the time, and he was super fit, which made what happened to him all the harder to understand. How can that happen when someone is so young, fit, and healthy?

Lucas waits while I lift the lid and peer inside, and then I gasp.

'Oh ...'

Inside the box are vintage decorations, and I take the box to the sofa and set it down on my lap.

'How did you remember these?'

'I spent enough time at your house growing up,' he says.

There are four Father Christmas figures not much bigger than my thumbs: one red, one blue, one pink and one green, all decorated with glitter. 'I used to love these figures.'

'I know.' He's smiling when I look at him, and something deep inside me flutters. This man is so thoughtful. It's crazy that he remembers things that mattered to me as a child. 'I remember you hanging them on the tree at your parents' house and thinking you were cute for taking such good care of them.'

'And the others.' Looking back in the box, I admire the two large baubles with open fronts, each one with a different snow-covered scene. A small boy sits on a sledge on one, his dog chasing after him. On the other, two reindeer stand on either side of a Christmas tree, the sky lit up with the North

Star, the snow shining with tiny flakes of glitter. 'They're so beautiful.'

'Not as beautiful as you.'

When I raise my eyes to him, everything blurs, and I know I am struggling to keep a hold of my emotions. This is too much on this my first Christmas without my husband. Memories rush in and assault me from over the years and my heart swells, then fractures into a million pieces. I lean over the box on my knees and sobs burst from me.

'Carla, what is it?' Lucas wraps a strong arm around my shoulders and pulls me close, his other arm around my knees, the box squashed between us. 'I'm so sorry. The last thing I wanted to do was to upset you.'

I cannot reply. I am crying hard now, my face scrunched up, my cheeks wet, the salty taste of my tears and snot filling my mouth. When he takes the box away and pulls me onto his lap, I wail. Finally, when my throat is raw and my eyes puffy, it's like my body has emptied itself of everything it has been holding inside and I am spent. Lucas takes charge, wipes away my tears and kisses my forehead, pushes my hair behind my ears. He holds me the way I need to be held. Supports me the way I have needed someone to support me. In his arms, I feel safe, cared for, secure.

As adults, we often have to be self-reliant and having a partner can help us feel less alone, but for the past ten months of my life in New York, I only had myself. After years of being part of a couple, it was just me and I was in shock. Nothing had prepared me for that fateful day. There had been no warnings, no rumblings of thunder to alert me to the storm that was coming, no way of knowing that everything was about to change and life would never be the same again. It destroyed my trust in life, in myself and in the world, and has left me teetering at the edge of a crevasse of vulnerability. I have skirted around it and tried to ignore it, and yet every single day I have been aware of it. Right in front of me. Waiting. Ready to consume me. And now, one thing has pushed me over the edge and into that crevasse and the shock of it is overwhelming and yet ... I am still here. I have been to the depths and survived. And while I went to the darkest depths, Lucas was there with me, holding me, keeping my head above water and being the friend I have needed since that awful day.

I never thought I'd know what it was like to feel safe again, but now I do, and it's all because of this wonderful man. This man whose arms are holding me tight right now. Even if I never feel this way again, I will be grateful to Lucas for giving me this moment. He has shown me that all is not lost. It is possible to find comfort in another, even if that person is not the man I loved with all my heart. Perhaps then, it will be possible to find love again? It's a thought I hadn't entertained and thought I never would, but this life can be long, it can be lonely, and it can be empty. Is it wrong to hope for love once more? To find a connection with another person that will be different to the one I had with Kofi, but once that can be fulfilling, nevertheless? Should I feel guilty for even entertaining that thought? What would Kofi want?

'Hey.' Lucas places two fingers under my chin and raises it so our eyes meet. 'I don't know exactly what you've been through, sweetheart, and I don't know if you can ever tell me. But I want you to know that I'm here for you. We all need someone to lean on and you can lean on me.'

The kiss that follows is soft as a butterfly's wings and I relax into it, allow myself to believe in this, in Lucas, in hope. In being here in the present and making the most of this moment because, after all, what else is there other than the here and now?

Chapter 32

Lucas

Christmas Eve has been a funny day for me for as long as I can remember. Going back to childhood, I'm sure there were years when it wasn't all bad, but try as I might, I can't recall them. I remember snippets of joy at Christmas time, like being allowed to add some chocolates to the shopping trolley at the supermarket and helping my mum to hide them at the back of the cupboard in the kitchen ready for Christmas Day. The excitement that came with that, as well as things like writing my letter to Father Christmas at school and also making Christmas cards for my parents, have stayed with me, but so have the unpleasant memories.

Perhaps it's part of the human condition for the bad to outweigh the good memories. Like the time I took home a card I'd made at school for my parents. The glitter dropped all over the carpet and it's a memory that makes me shudder. Even to this day, I have to be careful around glitter, because if I spill it anywhere — say if it comes off a card or one of those tree decorations I bought for Carla — then the flashbacks are awful. Another festive memory is of the annual Christmas concert at school when I waited for my parents to come and watch me. Realising that they weren't sitting in the audience — and that I was the only pupil in the school who didn't have anyone there at the end to take photos and hug me with pride — left me broken. That stuff stays with you and it's tough. It kind of put me off Christmas as an adult. Sure, I enjoyed the build up with the parties and extra opportunities to grab some female company, but as for the traditional celebrations, I couldn't be bothered. But this year, it's different. This year, Carla is here with me and I want it to be special for her. She deserves it.

As I make breakfast, I think about the past few weeks since Carla arrived in my world, and I can't quite believe the impact she's had. Two and a half weeks is little time wise, but in terms of the impact Carla has had on me, it's significant. It feels like far longer and I'm sure it's because we have a shared history and because she's not just some woman I met last night. That type of sex has its place and I'm grateful for the women I've spent time with over the years, but none of them has meant anything. Whereas Carla does. It's simple and clear and I like that it. Not that it's without fear, because I'd be mad to enjoy this time with her without worrying about what could go on at a deeper level, but we're both adults and we both have our baggage. However, I'm sure we can navigate our way through this so that when she leaves, we both survive with our hearts intact. It's doing us good, I'm sure it is, and that makes me want to spend even more time with her while she's here.

In the lounge, the lights on the tree twinkle, a welcome contrast to the gloom outside. It's cloudy but not snowing right now although I'm sure the mist is icy and I'm glad to be at home where it's warm and cosy. And where Carla is. I could've gone into the office this morning, but Edward and Jack no longer want to do so over the holidays because they're both happy and settled now, and so neither do I. There was a time when we'd all work whatever hours we could just to exist within the world of business and not think about our lives outside of the office, but it's funny what having a soft, warm body waiting for you at home can do to a man. Not that I'll ever want to surrender my career, but while I have Carla here, I don't want to miss out on being with her either. And so here I am, putting together a tasty festive feast to tempt her this morning while she sleeps in my guest room, possibly dreaming of snow and lights and what she wants me to do to her when she wakes.

I grab my phone and find a Christmas playlist, then send it to the TV speakers. Wham's *'Last Christmas'* fills the air, and it brings a smile to my face. Carla loved this song as a teenager and I can remember her singing along to it while she carried her Sony Walkman around, the headphones glued to her ears, unaware how loudly she was singing. As lovely as she is, her singing voice was not good back then and I doubt it has changed much now.

When the food is ready, I take it to the table then get the bottle of champagne from the fridge and pop the cork. I pour peach juice into flutes, then add champagne and check that the table looks perfect. I hope Carla likes what I've prepared because this is the first time I've ever made Christmas Eve breakfast for another person.

It's time to wake her up and to start our Christmas together. The clock is ticking and our time together is limited, but I want us to make the most of it and for Carla to have happy memories of her first Christmas in London.

Chapter 33

Carla

Lucas wakes me with a gentle kiss and I stretch out in the bed and smile up at him.

'Wakey wakey, beautiful,' he whispers.

'What time is it?' I ask as I sit up and yawn.

'Just after eight.'

'Early then?' I laugh because back in New York, my day would have started hours earlier as I set off just after dawn to clean hotel rooms. After eight is a luxury but this is my new life now and so I'm getting used to being able to sleep for longer. Not that I'm happy I had to start a new life at all, but it is what it is and I have to try to focus on the positives or I'll go mad. Whatever I might do to deal with what life has thrown at me, I am unable to turn back the clock to how things used to be.

'Do you want to sleep for longer?' he asks, and I can hear the hint of disappointment in his tone.

'No thanks. I'm hungry anyway.' As I stand up, I realise that I am hungry and it's good. For months I struggled with food, often making unhealthy choices because I was trying to find comfort in food and not caring about sustenance, but here in London, my appetite is returning.

'Well, that's good because I've prepared breakfast.'

'Let me quickly wash up and I'll join you.' I smile at him and my heart flutters at the sparkle in his blue eyes.

When I wrap my robe around me and head out to the lounge, my breath catches in my throat. Since I went to bed last night, Lucas has added more fairy lights to the room, draping them around the TV, the windows and the plants, as well as the kitchen island. It's gloomy outside, but the lights create a warmth indoors that easily banishes the gloom. Music is playing, and the familiar festive tunes that I've heard every Christmas for years and years make goose-bumps rise on my arms. As I walk past the tree, I spot the wrapped gifts underneath it and my chest squeezes. Lucas has gone all out to get things festive for our time together and a lump rises in my throat. How can I be so lucky as to get to spend time with this amazing man? He is so considerate and being here with him is healing my broken heart.

Lucas is standing near the table and has pulled out a chair for me.

'My lady,' he says as I sit down and he pushes the chair in.

The table is set beautifully with silver napkins and a matching table runner, and as I gaze at the effort he's gone to, tears prick my eyes. There's a platter of smoked salmon, gravadlax, lemon slices, and dill. There's a bowl of cooked prawns still in their shells and another bowl of what I'm guessing is salmon mousse. Lucas has also put out a plate of blinis and another of a variety of crackers.

'Is that caviar?' I ask as I point to the small glass bowl.

'It is. The very best caviar for you.'

'Wow.'

Lucas sits opposite me and picks up his flute. 'Here's to a very merry Christmas together. Thank you for the pleasure of your company, Carla.'

I clink my glass against his, then reply, 'The pleasure is all mine, Lucas. If you keep treating me this well, I won't want to leave.'

Our eyes meet.

There is a beat of silence as we both realise what I just said.

My heart seems to freeze in my chest and I try to swallow, but I'm worried I've ruined everything. The last thing a man like Lucas needs is pressure for more from a woman like me. A woman who has nothing to offer a man who already has everything.

Everything except love, a voice whispers in my ear, but I shake it off.

Lucas could have any woman he wanted any day of the week, and for him this is just a bit of fun. But I am grateful to him for doing all this for me because this Christmas would have been so awful if I'd been alone. Instead, I get to spend it here and to be spoilt by someone who does care for me. Albeit as a friend and part of what I'm guessing would be called a sexuationship these days.

'Thank you, Lucas. For everything. I'm really grateful. You've been incredibly kind and ...' I cough against the emotion in my throat. 'You have no idea how much this has meant ... this year of all years. I-I'll always remember your kindness.'

He looks down at the place setting in front of him and shakes his head. 'This is the most fun I've had in like forever, Carla, so don't think it's one way. You've been a delightful guest and we still have over a week left together to enjoy, so let's make the most of it.'

'Cheers to that.' I take another sip and the bubbles fill my mouth, then go straight to my head as the drink hits my empty stomach. I'd better fill up on salmon or I'll be drunk before lunchtime. But then again, why not? It is Christmas after all.

We eat and drink and soon my belly is full and we've drained the bottle of champagne. Lucas takes the dishes to the sink then returns with coffees and we move to the lounge and sit on the sofa. He pulls a soft throw over us both and I shuffle closer to him and rest my head on his shoulder.

'There's something deliciously decadent about being tipsy at this time of the morning,' I say with a giggle.

'I know what you mean,' he says. 'It's one of the good things about Christmas really, that day drinking is acceptable.'

We both laugh and he moves his arm so I can place my head on his chest. He's warm, and he smells divine and I feel a jolt of desire but also something else that makes me frown. Is it affection or something stronger? It's probably the booze and nothing to concern myself with. After all, I'm still in love with my husband, so how could I possibly fall in love with someone else? I mean, I know that Lucas isn't just anyone, but even so, I'm not ready to fall for someone else. Nowhere near ready. It would feel like I was betraying my marriage, and that's something I'd never want to do. Sex is one thing, a physical act to make myself feel better and help me to heal, and it's not like I went looking for it. Lucas kind of fell into my lap. I haven't fought this thing between us, but neither have I believed it to be anything more than it is. We're just two old friends sharing Christmas together and screwing while we're here together this snowy December in London.

'Carla,' Lucas says, and I turn to meet his eyes. His pupils dilate and I can see my reflection in them as if he's holding me captive inside his gaze.

'Yes?'

'Drink your coffee while it's hot.' He winks, and I force a smile to my face.

'Of course.' Inwardly, I shake myself. Here I am getting all deep and gooey and Lucas is still teasing me, still being the joker he always was. He's concerned with nothing more than making the most of a situation. There are no deeper feelings involved here than those of friendship and the primal urge to fuck the person he's sharing a space with.

But then he leans closer and presses a kiss to my forehead. My breath catches, because while I'm telling myself that this is not more to him, his actions suggest otherwise.

'Fancy watching a festive movie?' He reaches for the control and turns the enormous TV on, then flicks through the options.

'That would be great.'

A movie is perfect because it will allow me to relax and forget about all the complex things swirling around in my head. I can escape into someone else's life and watch as their story unfolds because, quite frankly, my own story is far too exhausting to work out right now.

So as *National Lampoons Christmas Vacation* starts, I snuggle closer to Lucas, sip my hot coffee and allow myself to let go of everything that's worrying me. There's time enough for worrying and second guessing everything other people do, but right now I'm going to get festive with the Griswolds.

'This is like my favourite movie ever,' I say.

Lucas gives me another forehead kiss before replying, 'I know. That's why I chose it.'

What the hell am I going to do with this man?

Chapter 34

Carla

Later that evening, Lucas tells me to get dressed in warm clothes because we're heading out. I frown at him because it's Christmas Eve, we've been relaxing all evening, and it's cold out, but he tells me to trust him.

When I'm dressed and have my coat, hat, and gloves on, he takes my hand and we ride the lift down to the ground floor. The security guard greets us and Lucas hands him an envelope that I assume is some kind of festive tip, then we walk out into the night.

It's snowing and the flakes catch the light as they drift down to the ground. I gaze up into the sky and feel them land on my cheeks and melt there like icy kisses from the heavens.

'Much as I'd like to stand there watching you do that, we'd better get a move on so we're not late.'

'Where are we going?'

'To welcome Christmas.'

'What?' My laughter echoes into the night as he takes my arm and we walk through the snow.

'We could catch the tube but it's a lovely evening so I think we should walk,' he says. 'I've allowed us enough time for that.'

We take just over twenty minutes to get to Trafalgar Square. It's beautiful there this evening, the ground covered with a light dusting of snow; the air filled with carols from a Salvation Army choir gathered between the fountains. Even though it's gone eleven P.M., people are milling around taking photographs and videos on their phones. I'm surprised because I thought most would want to be snuggled up at home with their loved ones right now, but then some don't have family to spend Christmas with and some people like being out and about on special occasions. I used to be happy just being at home with Kofi, but not everyone's the same.

'Did we come to listen to the carols?' I ask.

'We did, but not here.'

'Where then?' My brows meet as I try to work out what's going on.

'There.'

Lucas points across the square, and goosebumps rise on my skin.

'St Martin-in-the-Fields?' I ask.

'Yes. I have tickets for midnight mass.'

'You do?' My voice is filled with surprise because I didn't have Lucas down as religious.

'I don't attend church regularly, but there's something about midnight mass,' he says. 'I wasn't sure if you'd want to come, but it seems like the perfect way to welcome in our Christmas together.'

'Wow.' I am surprised but happy because this is such a sweet thing to do.

We climb the stone steps to the historical ecclesiastical building along with other people and a sense of magic fills the air. It's the magic of people coming together at a special time of year to celebrate life and the end of one year as we prepare for the next. Like Lucas, I'm not particularly religious — even though I did attend church with my parents as a child. Over the years, I stopped going because I was busy and I wasn't sure what I believed. Life became about getting through the days, paying the bills, and spending as much time as I could with Kofi. But the fact that Lucas has brought me here this evening means a lot because no man has ever taken me to midnight mass before.

We enter the church, and scents of pine and incense greet us. We are directed to our seats and when we sit down, I take the opportunity to have a look around.

The church is lit with candles set in sconces and chandeliers and at the front of the building; the choir stands ready in a semicircle. Behind them the altar is lit with more candles and spotlights dance around them creating the effect of falling snow. There is a sense of collective anticipation, and when Lucas takes my hand, my throat aches.

I hear the heavy doors to the church close and then the choir starts to sing and it is the most beautiful sound I have ever heard. They sing carols, including 'Away in a Manger',

'Good King Wenceslas', 'Hark! The Herald Angels Sing' and more. The service is moving, and I feel a part of something, united in a collective celebration of being alive, and it's only when Lucas hands me a tissue that I realise my cheeks are wet with tears. For so long I've felt isolated, bereft and without hope, and yet here in this moment, I am no longer alone.

Of course, as the choir sings 'Silent Night', my thoughts go to Kofi. It was his favourite carol and I close my eyes and allow myself to remember him. So much of life can be about moving on, healing and letting go, but I believe it's important to remember, to treasure the time we had together and to accept that I loved him and he loved me. While I will keep going, I will never forget him. He was a huge part of my life for so long and he will always remain in my heart and my mind. What happened was tragic and I miss him with every fibre of my being, but I am strong and resilient and I know from my time with Lucas that it is possible to feel joy again. It is possible to walk through a snowy evening and let the flakes melt on my cheeks and enjoy the sensation. It is possible to eat good food and drink good wine and enjoy them without feeling guilty about being alive. It is possible to make love to another man and enjoy reconnecting with my body and being present through every kiss, caress and sensation. Life is possible. It is there to be lived and since my arrival in London, Lucas has shown me that I can live again. I will always be thankful for this time with him because he has given me the gift of accepting that I am allowed to go on.

When people start to filter out of the church, I feel a sense of sadness because I don't want to leave. It has been a beautiful experience and I could happily stay there for hours and enjoy the sense of lightness the mass has given me.

When we reach the doorway, I say to Lucas, 'I'd like to light a candle if that's OK?'

'Of course.' He comes with me and I drop some money into the box, then take a candle and light it before setting it in the stand alongside the others. I take a moment to think of Kofi and to hold him in my heart, then I send him love.

When I turn back to Lucas, he takes my hand and we walk outside.

'Who's the candle for?' he asks.

'For my husband, Kofi.'

He nods. 'You're such a forgiving person, Carla.'

'Forgiving?' I ask as we stand at the top of the stone steps.

'Well yes,' he replies, a frown marring his brow. 'Lighting a candle for your ex shows what a kind and forgiving person you are.'

'Kofi isn't my ex.' I shake my head.

Lucas' frown deepens. 'You're still married? I mean, I know you were wearing the ring until recently, but I thought you'd separated because he let you down.'

My mind scans back through the past few weeks and it hits me that because I have not wanted to be the widow, I have not explained what happened to Lucas and he's been under the misapprehension that Kofi left me.

'Lucas,' I hold his gaze. 'My husband didn't cheat on me or leave me for someone else. My husband … he … he died.'

Starting Over With the Billionaire

I watch as Lucas' eyes widen and his lips part, then he pulls me against his hard chest. 'Fuck, Carla, I'm so sorry. I clearly misunderstood what had happened. I've been mad at Kofi for hurting you when it wasn't at all deliberate. It makes sense now because I couldn't understand how any man could ever bear to leave you.'

He holds me that way for a while, and I close my eyes and relax against him. People pass by, calling out Merry Christmas and the snow falls down around us and over the square. The Salvation Army sings 'O Holy Night' and it feels truly special to me.

And as Lucas holds me tight, I hear the softest whisper in my ear, a voice I have known for most of my adult life as well as I know my own, 'I'm OK, Carla. All is well now. You can let go.'

Chapter 35

Lucas

I wake in my own bed but I am not alone. Carla lies with her head on my chest. My arms are wrapped around her and as I listen to her relaxed breathing, something in my heart shifts. My eyes sting and I blink hard to clear them. Last night was intense. We went to midnight mass, and it was as beautiful as always, but this year it was even more special because Carla was with me. The way she immersed herself in the experience and witnessing how the music and service affected her really got to me. And then, finding out that her husband had not in fact left her as I had thought, but passed away, made me hurt for her.

When we got home, we talked for hours, and she told me all about waking one morning to find that Kofi had passed in his sleep. He was a young, healthy man in his prime, but death claimed him without warning, and since then she's been trying to piece her life back together again.

She has been carrying her grief for almost a year alone and yet she's still standing, still carrying on with that indomitable spirit of hers. I saw that spirit in her when she was a child and she'd stick up for herself whenever her brother teased her, and I saw it when she entered the pub three weeks ago. Carla is an incredible woman and I admire her with all of my heart.

And that is why letting her go next week is going to be so hard. I have never felt this close to a woman and I doubt I ever will do again. It's sad then that we have to go our separate ways, but I know what I'm like and I never want to be the reason Carla gets hurt. Plus, I thought she was a wounded wife before, but now I know she's a grieving widow and therefore, she has healing of her own to do. The last thing she needs in her life right now is a fucked-up complication like me. I won't bring good to her world, only more pain. I'm going to have to let her go, as much as it will hurt me to do so.

She stirs in my arms, and I tilt her chin and kiss her soft lips. 'Hey you,' I say. 'Merry Christmas.'

She smiles sleepily at me. 'Merry Christmas.'

When her hand slides down under the covers and takes hold of my ever-ready cock, I groan because I know this is going to be the best Christmas morning ever.

Chapter 36

Carla

Waking in Lucas' arms on Christmas morning is wonderful and I lie there breathing in his scent and listening to his heart beating. I have loved a man and know what it is to fall asleep with him, to stir in the night and feel his warmth at my side and to listen to the steady beating of his heart and hope it will go on forever. I have also known the pain of waking to find that man has passed in his sleep and that heart, one I deemed more precious than my own, had stopped. The man I thought I'd grow old with was gone, stolen from me while I slept in our bed, unaware that my life had changed overnight. What came next was a blur and I don't know how I got through it, let alone the days and weeks that followed. Grief cannot be cured; it is a relentless process that persists until one day, you awaken and realise the pain has lessened. The next day can be different again and so I also know that healing can be fickle. Grief will ebb and flow like the tide, it will be breathtakingly raw some days, others it will be numbed, and then there will be times when it will be present but like a cloud on the horizon, still there, but just far enough away so you can carry on with your day.

After midnight mass and hearing the voice outside the church — I'd like to think it was Kofi telling me he was OK, but it could have been my imagination — I have the cloud on the horizon feeling. I miss Kofi, but I am OK with that. I know it's all right to accept that I miss him and always will and yet to be here, alive, with Lucas.

When I slide my hand down and feel Lucas is ready as always, I can't resist taking hold of his shaft. I massage my hand up and down, feeling the silken sheath over steel. Lucas moans as I increase the speed of my hand and then slide on top of him and underneath the covers. I kiss his belly, trace the line of hair from his abdomen and down to the base of him, then lower. I cup his balls as I take the tip of his erection into my mouth and run my tongue over it, tasting his precum. It makes me ravenous for him so I use both hands to massage his length, feel him swelling under my grip and I take him deeper into my mouth and throat with each movement.

He's about to come when he stops my hands and stills my head, then he pushes me over onto my back and kneels over me. He takes hold of himself and masturbates while gazing down at me.

'Merry Christmas, indeed,' he says, his eyes filled with things that make my stomach flip over. The things he wants to do to me make me excited and yet nervous. Through our physical coupling I feel alive again and it's the only time when I am fully in the present.

Lucas leans over and runs the tip of his cock over my clit, tracing figure of eights until I pant with need.

'I want to see your ass jiggle,' he says, pulling me up and flipping me over onto my knees. I think he's going to take me doggy style, but he doesn't. Instead, he lies down and then lowers me onto his lap, sliding inside me as he pulls me into a sitting position with my knees against my chest. It pushes him deep and I suck in a breath to cope with the sensation. He moves in and out of me for a few strokes before reaching forwards and grabbing my ankles then tugging them so I'm astride him but facing away. 'Bounce for me, baby,' he growls.

That thick cock fills me as I bounce up and down. My heavy breasts sway from side to side and Lucas grips my bottom, squeezing the cheeks hard, then parting them so he can watch everything that's happening. It turns me on, but I need more friction, so while supporting myself with my left hand on his thigh, I touch my clit with my right and soon I am climbing towards the peak of arousal. Beneath my fingertips, the swollen bud grows hard and as I hear Lucas shout my name, I tumble over the edge of the abyss and am swallowed whole.

When Lucas has stopped pumping, he pushes me forwards so I am leaning on his legs, my breasts squashed between us and then he touches my sex. 'I like to see my cum in your pussy, to know that I made you wet and glistening and to see that you're still aroused.'

He pushes a finger inside me, and I shiver with little aftershocks of ecstasy, as if my body is keen to enjoy every ounce of the orgasms Lucas gives me.

'Keep my cum inside you where it belongs.' His voice is dark and low and it arouses me. This man has a way of making me feel in touch with the sexual side of me I didn't know was there. When I'm with him, I never feel ashamed of my sexuality and it's incredible to feel so free with who I am and what I want. Lucas wouldn't refuse me anything in the bedroom, I know and it's empowering.

Lucas slides out from under me and gets up off the bed then he reaches for my hand, pulls me towards him and helps me to stand. I go to reach for my robe, but he shakes his head and leads me out into the lounge. The room is cooler than the bedroom and my nipples pebble while goosebumps rise on my skin. He walks to the windows and pulls me towards him, then pushes me up against the glass. It's cold and I yelp, but he laughs.

'Feel everything, Carla, but don't fear it.'

He kisses me then, hard and rough, and bites at my lower lip before running kisses down my throat and over my collar bones. Cupping my breasts, he bites at them too, nipping hard enough at my nipples to make me gasp. He moves lower, trailing his big fingers over my skin until he reaches my thighs and then he parts them. When he touches my slit, I inhale sharply, then he slides two fingers inside me while rubbing my clit with the pad of his thumb. I'm still sensitive from my last orgasm, but his touch arouses me and I respond to him, wanting more.

When he pulls his fingers away, I whimper with disappointment, but then he takes hold of my thighs, lifts me in his powerful arms, and pushes me tight against the window. There is nothing between us and the street below other than the glass and while I know it's reinforced, it still excites me to know that there's an element of danger to this.

'I want to fuck you while London wakes up,' he says. 'I want the world to see how much I want you and for you to know how gorgeous you are.'

Between my legs, his cock hardens and soon finds its way inside me. He does as he promised, and it's not long before we both come, eyes locked, skin slick with sweat, bodies locked together.

When he withdraws from me, Lucas carries me back to the bedroom and lays me down on his bed, then pulls the covers over me. 'Rest now,' he says before heading into his bathroom.

I hear water running and him moving around in there and before long; he walks back into the bedroom. He's still naked, his heavy cock swaying between his legs, and I can't help but stare at it. He's like an addiction and I want more and more of him with every passing day.

'Come with me.' He holds out his hand, so I take it and he leads me into the bathroom where I see that his freestanding tub is filled with hot water and bubbles. I get in and sink under the water, then he climbs in and sits behind me, pulls me against his chest. Bubbles float up my skin, tickling over my thighs and between my legs and I lean back against Lucas and sigh with contentment.

Lucas grabs a bottle off the side, pours shampoo into his hands and massages it into my hair. It smells like apples and I become weak as his hands work all over my scalp. He washes it away using the shower head from the taps and then repeats the action. When it's squeaky clean, he adds a creamy conditioner to my strands and combs it to the ends with his fingers. By the time he's finished, I am physically weak and also emotional. No one has bathed me in what feels like a lifetime, but Lucas is taking care of me like I'm to be treasured and adored, and it's almost too much to bear.

'Hey,' he says, leaning forwards to peer at my face. 'Why are you upset? That was meant to be nice.'

'It was wonderful.' I sniff. 'But ...'

'But what, sweeting?'

'I-I'm afraid.'

'Why?' He puts his hands under my armpits and turns me so I'm lying on top of him.

'Because I know I can't get used to this. Because I know it has to end.'

He pulls me up so that I'm covering him like a human blanket and then he holds me tight against him, so tight I can barely breathe, but I don't care. I need him to hold me. I need to feel like I matter to him and that he cares. My heart is breaking because Lucas didn't deny that this will end. I knew what I was getting myself into from the start. Despite this, a tiny part of me had hoped Lucas might be the handsome knight I hadn't even known I needed to come and rescue me. Ironically, Lucas has given me hope while simultaneously stealing it away again.

Chapter 37

Carla

When we emerge from the water sometime later, Lucas wraps a towel around his waist then wraps a bath sheet around my body and a smaller towel around my hair. He takes me through to the bedroom and dries me off, then takes great pleasure in smothering me in luxurious body lotion that smells like vanilla. Body done, he rubs a rich moisturiser over my face and a coconut serum through my hair. I feel thoroughly pampered, and it almost sets me off crying again.

Lucas dries himself then puts on his robe and gets mine from my room and we go to the lounge and sit on the sofa. He puts a traditional carols playlist on his phone and sends it through the speakers by the TV and festive tunes fill the air.

'Time for some more champagne and gifts?' he asks, and I smile.

'You really didn't need to get me anything,' I say. 'You've done enough for me.'

'Like I was going to let Christmas pass by and not get you anything.' He winks. 'Indulge me. It's a pleasure to have someone to buy for who's not Edward, Jack or a member of their families.'

He goes to the tree and picks up several parcels and sets them down on the coffee table, then he heads to the kitchen. I hear him popping a cork and the tinkling of glasses as he gets them out of the cupboard. When he re-joins me, he hands me a glass of bubbly that I sip greedily. For some strange reason, I feel nervous and I'm hoping the alcohol will help.

'OK …' He looks at the gifts on the table, then selects one. 'Have this one first.'

I place my glass on the table, then accept the parcel and admire the pretty paper. 'Where's this from?'

'Harrods.'

'Did you wrap it?'

Lucas laughs loudly and his Adam's apple bobs. 'No, love. That's what shop assistants are for.'

I open the parcel carefully, afraid of tearing the pretty paper that I'm sure wasn't cheap, then I set it aside and gaze at the box in my hands.

'It's a smart watch.' Lucas helps me open the lid and then takes it out and puts it on my wrist. 'It's charged, so all you need to do is connect it to your phone.'

'Wow! This is too generous.'

Lucas shrugs. 'You deserve it. I thought it would help you get organised with your new life. Obviously, I didn't know exactly what had happened back then when I bought it, but I'm hoping it will still be a useful gift.'

'Lucas, it's perfect. Thank you so much!'

I throw my arms around his neck and hug him. He hugs me back and I feel his hands roam up and down my back, but then he shakes his head and pulls away. 'Sorry. I can't touch you without getting aroused. But I want you to open your gifts first.'

Nodding, I sit back, and he hands me another one. It's a new smartphone.

'To go with the watch,' he says.

'Oh Lucas.' My vision blurs and I swallow hard. 'This really is too much.'

'No, it's not. You're about to start over and these will help you. Besides which … I thought that if you want to message me and meet up or something going forwards, you'd be able to with these. I've paid the first three months of the phone contract ahead, but you can take it over then if you want to.'

I nod. 'I'll pay you back for the first three months as well.'

'No, you won't. It's part of the gift.'

The look in his eyes tells me he won't allow me to argue with him over this, so I don't even try. I'm getting to know when I can or can't change his mind, and this is one of the times when I can't.

I admire the watch, and new phone but then something occurs to me. Does he think he can message me whenever he wants a booty call? Is this what our relationship will be like going forwards? Can I exist like that? Only having him for the briefest of moments before he goes back to his life and I return to mine?

I am distracted then as he gives me the other gifts he bought me — some luxury spa products, an ivory silk robe and matching silk slip, and a freshwater pearl choker made of the prettiest little pearls strung on a silver chain with a pearl bracelet.

'I'm overwhelmed,' I say and I am. 'You've been so kind and I can't ever repay you for all this.'

'Carla, I told you it's my pleasure, and it is. I enjoyed shopping for you and being able to spoil you. I could easily have bought more, but had to restrain myself because I didn't want to make you uncomfortable.'

'I got you something, too.' Standing, I pad across the room and through to my bedroom, then I retrieve the gift from in the wardrobe where I hid it last week after a solo shopping trip. I return to Lucas and sit next to him, then hold out the gift.

'Oooh. What is it?' He waggles his eyebrows.

'It's something I hoped you might like. I was trying to decide what I could get the man who has everything and—'

'Everything?' He frowns.

'Well, yes. You have so much money you can buy anything you want and so I thought—'

'Not everything. Money can't buy you honesty or love or loyalty.' He rubs at the back of his neck, and I watch him curiously. 'It can't buy you caring parents or a secure childhood or turn back the clock.'

His voice cracks and I reach out and take his hand. 'Lucas, what is it? What happened to you?'

He shakes his head and assumes the smile I know so well, but I know he's faking it. His eyes show his anguish and a muscle in his jaw is twitching.

'Nothing,' he says tightly. 'Nothing at all.'

'It's not nothing because the things you just said are—'

'Nothing. I've had a few drinks this morning, and it's an emotional day knowing what I do about you and ... that's all. Can we just forget I said anything?'

'Of course.' I nod. 'But please remember I'm here if you ever want to talk.'

'Sure.'

'So...' I inject enthusiasm into my tone. 'I was looking for an original gift and this came to mind.'

I hand him the gift and he smiles at me. 'Thanks, Carla.'

'My pleasure.'

I hold my breath while he unwraps the paper I chose and then the tissue paper and holds up the book. 'An illustrated hardback edition of *A Christmas Carol*?' It's a question and I bite the inside of my cheek. Have I screwed up?

'Don't you remember?'

He gazes at the book, and I watch as he blinks and then realisation dawns on his face. 'Yes! I do. You were about ... twelve or thirteen?'

'Thirteen.'

Starting Over With the Billionaire

'And you had to write a summary of the story for school.'

'But I was struggling...'

'And you asked Dane, but he didn't have the time, so I helped you.'

'You did. I only remembered last week when I was browsing in a bookshop, but you sat with me and helped me to write that summary and I got an excellent grade for it.'

'I love this story!' His smile meets his eyes now and my heart swells.

'I remember you telling me that.'

'Shall we read it together?'

'OK.'

The intercom interrupts us, and he grabs his phone. 'But first we need to eat.'

'To eat?' I'd clean forgotten about Christmas dinner.

'Hold on.' He goes to the lift and waits for a few seconds, then presses the button to open the doors. A man dressed as a server pushes a large, wheeled trolley like they use in hotels for room service out of the lift. 'Thank you, Arthur. I'll take it from here.' Lucas hands the man an envelope and says, 'Merry Christmas to you and your family.'

'Why thank you, Mr Barrett.' Arthur smiles, then waves at me. 'Merry Christmas, Miss.' He gets back in the lift and the doors close.

Lucas pushes the trolley over to the kitchen area and says, 'Are you hungry?'

'I am now I can smell that.' My stomach gives a little rumble and I get up and go to the table where Lucas is setting out plates of food and removing the steel covers.

'Seeing as how it's Christmas Day, I ordered in from a local hotel.' Lucas gestures at the table where plates of steaming food sit, making my mouth water. There's a plate of sliced turkey breast with a side of stuffing, another with roast potatoes and bowls of various vegetables, including carrots, broccoli, red cabbage, cauliflower cheese and more, as well as a jug of thick brown gravy.

'It looks delicious.'

'Well, sit down and tuck in.'

We sit and I eat and eat until my stomach feels fit to burst. Through dinner, Lucas tops up our champagne and we talk and laugh and relax together. When we've finished, my new phone rings. Lucas even transferred my number to the new contract. It's my parents and brother to wish us both a Merry Christmas. They're keen to speak to Lucas too and Dane says they must have a catch up when he's next in the UK.

I go to clear the plates, but Lucas shakes his head. 'Leave them for now. Let's have a brandy to burn a hole in all that food and we can read my gift.'

Ten minutes later, we're snuggled up on the sofa, cut-glass tumblers in hand, a blanket over our knees and Lucas is holding his copy of '*A Christmas Carol*'.

'Ready?' he asks.

'Ready.' I rest my head on his shoulder, and he starts to read...

Chapter 38

Lucas

Christmas comes and goes in a blur of making love, eating good food, and sipping champagne, and I enjoy my time with Carla so much that when the New Year bells chime, and I realise our time together has almost come to an end, I feel a sense of dismay. I knew this was only temporary, but I've got used to having her around and so knowing that she's going to leave is hard. I helped her pack her things yesterday on New Year's Day, and I've arranged for my chauffeur to take her to the station later, but waking on this — our last morning together — is making my chest feel hollow.

I sneak out of bed and go and make coffee, then bring it to Carla in bed. She's sleeping on her back, her hair spread across my pillow, and I take a mental snapshot of her. I'm going to miss waking up next to her and being able to hold her beautiful curves against me.

Her eyes open, and she blinks up at me. 'Morning.'

'Good morning, beautiful.' I put the coffees on the bedside table and slide back under the covers.

'What time is it?' she asks, then yawns.

'Still early.'

'Good.' She echoes my sentiments.

I brush her hair away from her face and kiss her lips, her cheeks, her forehead, her small ears. I bury my face in her hair and inhale its scent of apple and vanilla and the smell that's uniquely hers and that drives me crazy. When she wraps her hands around my erection, I shiver with pleasure and move on top of her, needing to be inside her. I wriggle out of my pyjama bottoms and lie between her soft thighs, so my cock presses against her wet heat.

Over the past few days, I've thought about this moment and what will effectively be our final time having sex. I imagined all the positions we could try, but now that the moment is here, all I want is to gaze into her beautiful eyes and be inside her one last time.

She takes my shaft and guides me inside her inch by delicious inch and soon her warmth is wrapped around me. I pause there, savour the sensation of being bareback inside her and of feeling her underneath me, open to me. I lean on my elbows and kiss her gently, trying to make this time last because I don't think it can ever happen again. It's not that I didn't consider a friends with benefits scenario for us long-term, but I think Carla might grow to want more. I simply can't give her more than this, so as hard as it will be, I have to let her go.

Chapter 39
Carla

When Lucas got up this morning, I wanted to beg him to come back to me so the night would never end, but I didn't. Instead, I feigned sleep and then when he returned with coffees, I pretended to wake up for the first time. I struggled to sleep last night because today is the day that our sexuationship comes to an end. Today is the day I return to my childhood home and try to pick up the pieces of my life. It's going to be so hard and I don't know how I'm going to walk out of here, but I also know that I have no choice. As much as I would like to stay here with Lucas, I need to find my feet in this world as a single woman, and I need to have some space. Lucas has made it clear that this is nothing more than two old friends having sex while under the same roof, and that's just fine. He was clear about it from the start. I know he has something holding him back from commitment and although I've tried to encourage him to share, he's remained silent and that's his prerogative.

I'm glad when Lucas gets back into bed and wonder what he's got planned for us this morning, but he when makes love to me in the missionary position, it's incredible. He's between my legs, supporting his weight on his arms, but with that magnificent cock deep inside me. I can feel every glorious inch filling me up and making me feel whole.

He doesn't move for a while and my core flutters around him because I'm aroused just having him inside me. His eyes are dark and I feel him pulsating each time my sex squeezes him. It's not long before I feel the ripples of orgasm starting in my clit and spreading out in delicious waves of pleasure. Lucas' eyes widen and then he thrusts three times and groans as he comes too.

'I'm sorry,' he says, his eyes filled with sadness. 'I wanted to make that last, but I could feel your excitement and it was too much.'

'Don't be sorry. That was beautiful,' I reply and as I blink, a tear runs down my cheek and soaks into the pillow.

'It really was.' He kisses me then gently pulls out of me and moves behind me so he can spoon me.

'Thank you for letting me stay,' I whisper.

'Thank you for staying. You have no idea how much I've enjoyed having you as my guest.'

We stay that way for some time as the light from the lounge becomes brighter in the hallway and our coffee goes cold. This time with Lucas has been wonderful.

I will always remember us this way, but I also know that it's time for me to start the next chapter of my life.

Nothing, not even this, can last forever...

Chapter 40

Carla

I ask Lucas not to come down to the limo with me because I can't face saying goodbye there. He comes down in the lift to help me with my bags, then he heads back up to his apartment. I get into the back of the limo with my case and bag, then look up at the building one last time. My heart is racing and I'm scared that I won't see Lucas again, but then I remind myself that I need to do this; I need to stand on my own two feet and start over.

As the driver pulls away from the kerb, I take a deep breath and try to prepare myself to embark upon my new life.

My phone pings, so I open my handbag and pull it out, expecting to see a text from Lucas. My heart jumps as I unlock my phone, wondering if he's going to ask me to come back, but it's not from him, it's from Ava asking if I could meet her and Grace ASAP.

I reply telling her I'm on my way to the station and she comes back immediately to invite me to the office she rents with Grace because they have a proposition for me.

Life sometimes does this. It offers us a choice, and this is mine: go back to Devon and start my new life there or find out what Ava and Grace want. I've booked my train tickets and if I don't get to the station in an hour, I'll miss the train, but I'm curious. If I don't take this chance, then I could be turning my back on something that is meant to be.

I ask the driver to take me to the office instead of the station, then sit back and sigh. If I claimed that I wasn't sad to be leaving Lucas, I'd be lying, but I'm also filled with a sense of hope. I have lost so much and yet I have gained too, and so today I am happy to go with the flow and find out what opportunities lie ahead for me. Only then can I make an informed decision about what I do next. If life has taught me anything so far, it's that nothing is guaranteed, but anything is possible, whether good or bad. I will pin my knickers to my vest, take this next step and see where it leads me.

THE LIMO PULLS UP in front of *Amazing Grace Weddings* on Salem Road and I get out and reach for my suitcase. The driver tries to help me, but I shake my head and wave him away. After I've thanked him and told him I'll make my own way to the station later, he wishes me luck then drives away.

Notting Hill is such a pretty area and I can see why Ava and Grace wanted to open their office here. I push open the door to the office and pull my case inside, then look around. The open-plan space is light and airy, with a desk to my right, then two more at the rear. The floorboards are sanded and there are circular lights above my head and sash windows with grey frames. Pinboards on the walls feature displays of wedding dresses and veils, suits and top hats, images of cakes and favours as well as possible venues and table settings. It's chic, stylish and professional.

'Carla!' Ava waves at me as she appears through a doorway at the back of the room. 'I'm so glad you came.'

She walks over to me, and I take in her black wool maternity dress with black leather ankle boots. She's wearing a gold necklace with a heart locket and gold hoops in her ears. Her brown hair is pulled into a messy bun on top of her head. Her makeup is minimal, but I don't think she needs much anyway because she has that pregnancy glow I've heard people talk about.

'Hi,' I say with a smile.

'Come and have a seat.' She takes my hand and then looks at my case. 'Let me put that out of the way for you.'

'No! It's OK, I can do that. You shouldn't be moving anything heavy.'

She laughs. 'Not you as well! Between Edward and Joe, I'm not allowed to lift a thing at home. They're both being so protective and treating me like I'm made of glass, but I keep telling them that I'm pregnant, not ill.' She laughs and I watch her beautiful face light up with love as she speaks about her family.

She leads me to a seating area near one of the rear windows and I tuck my case to the side of one of the sofas, then sit down. Ava sits opposite me, then springs back up. 'Where are my manners? Can I get you a drink?'

'I'm fine, thanks.' Shaking my head, I fold my hands in my

lap and try to relax my shoulders because I feel like they're sitting right beneath my ears.

'Hello! Sorry I'm a bit late!' Grace has come through the front door along with a rush of cold air. She removes her coat as she walks over to us. 'I popped to see my aunt and you know what she's like when she gets chatting.' She gives Ava a knowing look and Ava nods. 'But she did send some cakes for us.'

Grace holds up a small box, and Ava licks her lips. 'Please tell me they're her triple chocolate brownies?'

'Yes, they are! She knows how much you love them.'

'Maisie is a diamond!' Ava reaches for the box and opens it, then gazes inside. 'You have to try one of these.' She offers me the box, but I shake my head.

'I'm fine for now, thanks.' Truth be told, I'm far too nervous to eat and I suspect a brownie would get lodged in my throat.

Grace sits next to Ava and drapes her coat over the back of the sofa, then runs her fingers through her long blonde hair. 'Right then ... to business ...' She fixes her green eyes on me and Ava does the same, although I think she has to make an effort to drag her amber gaze away from the brownies first. 'Now, we know you have a train to catch, but we've been talking and we have a proposition for you.'

'OK.' I swallow but my mouth is dry, and I wish I had accepted Ava's offer of a drink.

'It's why we've come into the office today. We had planned on staying closed for two weeks over the holidays, but when we got talking about this yesterday, we decided we had to speak to you before you left for Devon.'

I look down and notice that my hands have clenched into fists, so I spread my fingers over my lap and take a slow breath. The suspense here is hard to take, but I'm sure there must be a good reason for them asking me to come in today.

'Yes ...' Ava smiles. 'The thing is, Carla, our business is expanding rapidly and we're incredibly busy already. There are plenty of people wanting to get married despite what the media might say about marriage going out of fashion, and so we need to take on more employees.'

'Right.' I look from Ava to Grace and back again.

'We know from what you said at Christmas that you haven't got a job yet, and we also know that you have HR experience, so we wondered if you'd be interested in joining the team.' Ava's eyes widen as she looks at me and I try to keep my expression neutral.

'We'd need to get references from your employer in New York and to go through things in more detail, obviously,' Grace says, 'but you worked for the charity for a long time. We were both impressed with what you told us you'd achieved when we spoke at the party.'

'But the crucial question then is whether you'd like to work with us at *Amazing Grace Weddings*,' Ava adds. 'It's not everyone's cup of tea and for all we know you might have other things planned already, but we couldn't let the opportunity pass by without asking you first.'

They both smile at me and then Grace stands up. 'I think perhaps you need some water, Carla?'

I nod so she goes over to a water cooler and fills a cup, then brings it to me. I sip the water and sigh inwardly with relief. My throat was parched.

'When ummm ... would this job start?' I ask when I can speak again.

'As soon as possible. See ...' Ava rubs her belly. 'I don't want to work right until I pop, so the sooner we can get our ducks in a row, the better for all of us.'

'I'm the same.' Grace places her hands on her stomach and nods. 'We've already employed two other people so we can train them before we go off on maternity leave, but we still have the HR vacancy and one other role to fill.'

I sip my water and place the cup on the low table in front of me.

'How about we email you the job spec, salary and pension info and you can have a think about it?' Ava asks. 'Let's go through to the back for a moment and give Carla some space, shall we?' Ava tugs at Grace's hand.

They both get up and head out the door at the rear of the office and I am left alone. For some reason, I am suddenly overwhelmed with emotion, so I reach for my bag and slide my hand into the side pocket for the pack of tissues I always keep in there. Instead, I pull out a small card. It's one of those inspirational quote cards and when I see it, my heart squeezes because I haven't seen this in ages. Kofi bought it for me in the early days of our relationship when I was trying to take things slowly with him but falling madly in love despite my best efforts.

I hold the card up and read it even though I know what it says.

You only regret the chances you don't take.

I hear Kofi reading it to me when he was asking me to take a chance on him and on starting a life with him in New York. It was such a big deal for me. Making a commitment and opening my heart to let him in was scary, but I did it and look at what I gained from our time together. We shared so much love and so many wonderful times and I know that despite what happened, I would never change a thing about our life together. Finding this card now, it's like he's here with me, encouraging me to take a chance. If someone has placed this opportunity in my lap, then I should grab it with both hands. It's not something I'll regret if I try it, but I could well regret not giving it a go.

So when Ava and Grace return to the sofa opposite, I smile at them both then say, 'I've had a think about your offer and I'd love to accept. I know you need references and there's paperwork to be dealt with, but this is a chance I'd love to take and I hope you'd like to take a chance on me.'

Before I know what's happening, Ava and Grace have come over to me and they both lean over their bumps and hug me. They are so kind and welcoming, and it reaches down to something inside me and makes my heart open up like a flower to the sun.

'Can I ask why?' I croak out.

'Why what?' Grace frowns.

'Why you're being so kind to me?'

Ava licks her lips, then says, 'Look, Carla, we've both been through tough times in the past but we were given a chance to start over. I see something of me in you, of how I used to be. I was given a helping hand and I'd like to pass that on.'

'Me too.' Grace nods. 'Life is tough and we all get battle scars along the way, but kindness can help us to heal.'

'Did Lucas tell you …' I leave the question unfinished, but they both look away and so I know. Lucas told them about Kofi and my loss and while I could feel annoyed because he shared this information with them, I don't because I know he wouldn't have said anything maliciously. It would have been because he trusts them and they are friends, and friends share these types of things.

'Lucas told Edward because he was upset for you,' Ava says. 'He's very fond of you.'

'He really is,' Grace adds.

'He's a good man.' I push my shoulders back and try not to let the pain of leaving him this morning swell again inside my chest.

An hour later, after we've gone through some details and I've confirmed that I am definitely interested in joining the team, we are standing near the front door of the office. 'I guess that I'm going to need to look for somewhere to live.'

'We can help you with that,' Grace says. 'My aunt has a room you could rent until you find somewhere more permanent.'

'Actually, I have a spare room.' The voice sends shivers down my spine, and I turn. I didn't even hear the door opening, but there he is.

Tall. Broad. Handsome. His salt and pepper hair shining under the lights. He's wearing a dark jacket with indigo jeans and boots and his piercing blue eyes are fixed on me like there's no one else in the room.

'Lucas.' His name is a whisper on my lips and yet it has the power to make my heart sing.

'Excuse us a moment,' Ava says and I hear her and Grace walking away and I am left alone with Lucas. It feels like weeks since I saw him last, but it's only been hours.

'Can we talk?' he asks.

'Of course.'

'I shouldn't have let you leave this morning without speaking to you about ... some things.'

I am lost for words because I can't take all of this in. Lucas has come to find me and he wants to speak to me. I had thought I might never see him again and yet here he is.

'Will you hear me out, love?' He holds out a hand and I take it.

'Of course I will. But ... how did you find me?'

His eyes are shining and I realise that he's feeling emotional, too.

'My driver. I asked him if he'd dropped you at the station, but he said you wanted to come here. Shall we get a coffee?'

'Yes.'

I look back to the doorway at the rear of the office and see Ava and Grace standing there, grinning like they've just won the lottery. I give them a wave and make a phone of my hand, so they know I'll call them, then I step out into the chilly London afternoon with Lucas, my heart beating out his name.

Chapter 41

Lucas

Carla and I sit at a table in the coffee shop on the corner that's a short walk from *Amazing Grace Weddings*. I knew where to find her today because my driver told me where he'd dropped her off. After she left my apartment, I was planning on heading to the office to get some work done. I planned on immersing myself in spreadsheets so I wouldn't have to feel the pain of seeing her leave, but when he came to collect me, I had to ask about her. How was she when he dropped her at the station? Did she seem happy? Did she ask him to pass on a message? Pathetic perhaps, but I can't seem to help myself when it comes to her. But then he told me she'd asked him to take her to the office on Salem Road and that was it. I told him to take me there too. My heart knew what it wanted to do all along, and my brain just needed to catch up.

And now here we are. I know that Ava and Grace have offered Carla work because I phoned Edward on my way to *Amazing Grace Weddings*. Edward told me what Ava and Grace had planned. It's kind of funny really because

Starting Over With the Billionaire

Ava and Grace have teased me a lot about being single and told me that when I met the one, I'd know. They said that I'd change my mind and settle down and I laughed at them. How I laughed! But here I am, being led by my heart and admitting, albeit reluctantly, that they were right.

I pick up my coffee and take a sip, then put the mug back down and cup my hands around it. I want to hold Carla's hand, but I also need to give her some space while I tell her what I need to say. For all I know, she doesn't feel the same way about me as I do about her and in that case I cannot put any pressure on her at all.

'Carla,' I say, my pulse thundering in my ears. 'I enjoyed the past few weeks with you so much.'

'As did I with you.' She smiles but I see something in her eyes that makes me wonder if I'm about to do the right thing. It's like the openness that I've got used to seeing there has been replaced with a wariness and it saddens me.

'I umm ... I know it hasn't been long, but I also know that I have powerful feelings for you.'

She blinks. Opens her mouth as if to say something, then closes it again.

'I don't want to put any pressure on you to say you feel the same because I–I don't feel I'm worthy of you. There you were, happily married and then you lost your husband and here I've been ... sleeping with a different woman every week, sometimes more than one a week and—'

Her audible inhalation makes me wince. It's not something I'm proud of and I feel regret now that I behaved like that, but going from woman to woman meant that I didn't develop feelings for any of them.

'And I was acting like I didn't care, like I'd never care, but then ... you walked back into my life and I can't deny that you've changed me.'

'I've changed you?'

Nodding, I take another sip of my coffee. 'You have. I'm fucked up though. I don't feel worthy of you, but even so I have to know how you feel because otherwise I'll drive myself mad.'

'Lucas, please tell me. I know there's something you've been afraid to share, but I promise you there's no judgement here.'

I inhale deeply. 'My childhood wasn't what I claimed it was. Growing up, I loved my parents, but they weren't exactly a model mum and dad. I feel guilty even admitting it because who wants to say bad things about their parents? I knew seeing how your parents were with you and Dane that my childhood was different. Your parents loved you, worried about you and would do anything for you, but mine... They were barely there and when they were I felt like I annoyed them and they disapproved of me. Nothing I could do made them proud, and it was tough. I yearned for their approval, for them to tell me they were proud of me and that they loved me, but it never happened.'

'Oh god, Lucas, I'm so sorry.'

'That's the thing though ... I don't want you to pity me. I'm not one to wallow in self-pity. I'm successful and I've done well for myself. I have more money than I need and yet ...

it's like whatever I do, I can't escape my past. Even now, there are days when I wish they'd let me know that they're proud of where I am and who I am, but I know it won't happen.'

'There's a little boy inside you still.' She holds my gaze, her beautiful grey eyes filled with compassion.

'I guess so.' Heat flushes my cheeks because I feel embarrassed admitting it.

'There's a little girl inside me too, Lucas. We might grow up, but we're still the same people inside. We all have vulnerabilities.'

Just when I thought this woman couldn't be more amazing, she shows me this much understanding. 'Fuck, Carla, you're like the most incredible person I've ever met.'

'I'm just human. I've experienced pain and I know it comes in all sorts of forms. Not having parents who are there for you is a major issue. Don't forget, I worked for a children's charity and so I understand how damaging neglect can be.'

I rub my face hard. The shame of not being loved by your parents runs deep. It's like hot lava bubbling in your gut. You can ignore it, paper over it, but eventually it's going to rush to the surface and explode like a volcano.

'My mum walked out when I was thirteen.'

I look up and see that Carla's eyes are glistening.

'I didn't tell anyone. My dad was still there and yet not really there because he drank a lot and went out a lot and so I often had to fend for myself. It was tough, but I found solace in learning and I worked hard at school, then hard at college so I could get the scholarship for university. Since graduation, I've thrown myself into my work. It's the one thing that can't hurt me or abandon me. But being with you, it made me realise what I've been missing out on. My fear has stolen away years when I could have been more fulfilled, when I could have had someone in my corner if I'd just been prepared to take a chance.'

'But taking a chance on someone is scary, right?' she asks.

'Terrifying.'

'Because that person might leave you like your mum did?'

'Yes.'

I brush the back of my hand over my cheeks to wipe away the tears that escape.

'Have you seen your mum since she left?'

'No. Nor do I want to. In fact, I don't even know if she's alive now. What could she possibly say that would change what happened? What she did to a teenaged boy who loved her and needed her but whom she abandoned?'

Carla gets up and comes around the table and wraps her arms around me. I lean into her, breathing in her perfume and her own wonderful scent. And then it hits me. Carla, for me, is like coming home. She is everything I never had and now everything I want and need. I am in love with her.

'Lucas ... I'm not going anywhere.'

I look up at her and she holds my face in both her hands.

'Lucas ... I love you.'

'I love you too.' It's only been weeks since she came into my life again, but during that time I have felt more for her than for anyone else my entire adult life. What we have shared has opened me up to the hope that I could love and be loved. 'It can only be you for me, Carla. No one else will be right. But you've been through so much and I don't want to put pressure on you. I know you're still grieving for your husband and I'd never expect you to deny that.'

'I will always grieve for Kofi because I loved him, but that doesn't mean I don't have room in my heart to love you too. The time we spent together has helped me to see that. I never thought to feel for another man, but the way I feel when I'm with you means I don't want to walk away from this either.'

'So what do we do?' I ask.

She takes my hand and pulls me up, then she kisses me. Her body moulds against mine and I hold her tight, knowing that this is it for me. Now she's told me how she feels, I'm never going to let her go.

'Lucas,' she says, grabbing the handle of her suitcase with her free hand while still holding on to me. 'Now, we go home.'

We leave the cafe together and step out into the chilly January morning. At last, I can open my heart to a woman because finally, I've found the woman who has the key to my heart.

And when I really think about it, it's clear as day that Carla had the key all along.

EPILOGUE – Carla – 8 months later

Standing on the stone steps of the old Marylebone Town Hall, we smile at the photographer. Lucas holds my hand tight, and I keep snatching glances at him. He looks handsome today in a navy suit that complements his eyes and a silver-grey tie that matches mine. I'm wearing a silver dress with a shirred waist and the pearl necklace and bracelet Lucas bought for me, and I have pearl clips holding my hair up. The hairdresser pinned my hair up in a French plait, then added the clips, but she styled curls to fall around my face and the nape of my neck. More than once Lucas has kissed my nape, telling me how sexy I look and how much he wants me.

To my right, Ava and Edward stand together with Joe, and Ava cradles their six-month-old baby girl, Hester. To my left, Grace, and Jack each hold one of their twin boys, Roman, and Rafferty, who've just turned five months.

Behind the photographer, my parents stand with family and friends of ours, and my brother, Dane, keeps flashing grins at me. When I told him Lucas and I were getting married, he laughed and said he knew it would happen one day. I asked what he meant, and he said it was always on the cards the way I trailed around after Lucas when I was younger. It's not exactly a flattering image of myself to have, but I don't mind because I think he's right; I did always have a soft spot for Lucas, but I needed to be an adult in order to allow the seeds that were planted all those years ago to grow.

Talking of seeds ... I was so busy with my new job and settling into my new home — i.e. Lucas' luxury apartment — that I forgot about getting my contraceptive implant changed. It was only when I felt queasy in the mornings that I thought something might be wrong. I told Lucas, and we bought a pregnancy test together and did it as soon as we got home. I'm now twelve weeks along, but no one else knows yet because we wanted to keep it between us until after the first scan. Whenever he thinks no one's looking, Lucas tenderly touches my stomach, and he's constantly attentive, making sure I'm feeling OK and asking if I need anything. Ava and Grace have both told me on numerous occasions that Lucas is a changed man and it's all because of me. I'll take that though, because I know I've changed because of Lucas. I felt hopeless when I arrived in London, but now I feel like I have everything I've ever wanted and then some.

When the photographer has finished, we all make our way to the reception at the Savoy. We could have married there too, but there was something about the town hall that seemed so attractive to me and these days I'm all for trusting my gut instincts.

After our arrival at the Savoy, Lucas tells the wedding planners — Ava and Grace — that we're going to pop to our room before joining everyone, and they both smile knowingly. He seems agitated in the lift and when we get to the fifth floor; he leads me towards our wedding night suite. Ava and Grace both know what room he's booked and I've been desperate to find out, but they refused to tell me.

'You booked the Royal Suite?' My mouth falls open as we enter the rooms that span the entire riverside of the fifth floor of the hotel. I stand before the windows that offer panoramic views of the Thames and London landmarks; my heart filled with awe. I don't think I'll ever take the sheer amount of money Lucas earns for granted and I'll never get used to the luxury. That's not to say I won't enjoy it, though.

'Only the best for my wife,' he says, coming to stand behind me.

I feel how hard he is, and it sends a shiver of delight through my body. The pregnancy hormones have made me hornier than usual, and Lucas has been only too happy to cater to my every whim. When he crouches down and lifts the hem of my dress up to my thighs, then presses his face against my bottom, I moan with need.

Lucas turns me around and gives me my dress to hold, then nuzzles my sex through the ivory silk panties and soon they're soaked. I lean against the windowsill as he peels them down my legs, then he kisses my smooth mound and runs his clever tongue over the folds, tracing slow circles on my clit. The bud swells under his tongue and when he slips two fingers inside me, my body shudders as an orgasm seers through me and I grab his head and pull him against me so I can take every spasm of pleasure from his tongue.

Lucas stands and kisses me, then lifts me in his arms and carries me from the morning room to the bedroom. The bed is a grand fourposter with a gold and cream silk canopy. The dark wood frame of the bed is intricately carved in gold, and the room is spacious enough to fit my entire New York apartment.

As my new husband lays me down on the bed, I stretch out and luxuriate in the comfort and in his love. He removes his jacket and tie, then he comes to me and arranges the skirt of my dress so he can look at me. He loves to do this and I love to let him.

'Now then, Wife,' he says, 'We'd better consummate this marriage so there'll be no escaping me.'

The look in his eyes is one of love and possession, and it sends a thrill through me. The fact that he's so protective and devoted is something I treasure, and I know I'd be lost without him now. He gives me all the room I need to grow, but he's always there when I need him. I could ask anything of him and he would do it in a heartbeat.

He kneels between my legs and frees his impressive erection, then he holds it as he enters me. I wrap my legs around his waist and sigh as he fills me in the way he was always meant to do. He moves slowly at first and I tighten around him, holding him inside me and enjoying the sensation of being filled with him. Our mutual pleasure builds quickly as he increases his pace and soon I am gripping hold of his shoulders. I rise to the peak of pleasure then crash over the edge, over and over again, like waves pounding against the shore. Lucas joins me and I feel his hot seed as it fills my core and then we lie there still joined, our breathing in sync, our hearts beating as one.

'Should we join our guests, Wife?' he asks after he's pulled out of me and tidied us both up.

'I think perhaps we should.' I giggle as I fluff out the skirt of my dress and pin up some tendrils of hair that escaped during our lovemaking.

He offers me his arm and I take it as we walk through the beautiful apartment, but right now I only have eyes for Lucas and I know he only has eyes for me. Lucas has played a major role in my healing journey. There are still decisions to be made, such as whether he will try to find out what happened to his mother and whether to contact his father, but they are things I can help him with just as he has helped me. I am convinced now that there is nothing I can't do with this man at my side. My lover, my best friend and my husband are all rolled into one gorgeous package.

We step out into the hallway and let the door close behind us, and I relish the significance of the moment as I prepare to start over with my very own billionaire.

The End

IF YOU ENJOYED STARTING *Over With the Billionaire*, why not read the other books in this gorgeous series *Meeting the Billionaire Boss* and *Healing the Billionaire's Heart*? Also, give my page a follow http://amazon.co.uk/Wynter-Wilde and you can find out about new releases and offers.

Dearest Reader,

I hope you enjoyed *Starting Over With the Billionaire*. It was a lot of fun to write but also very emotional as Carla and Lucas had to overcome their inner conflicts to be able to heal and find their Happy Ever After.

If you enjoyed the story, please consider leaving a rating and a short review because reviews are so helpful to us authors in terms of visibility and helping other readers decide whether to try our books. Also, if you follow my page here - http://amazon.co.uk/Wynter-Wilde - you'll be able to find out what's coming next and I'll have plenty more stories coming your way soon!

For now, I wish you good health and happiness.

With love, Wynter xx

Also from Wynter Wilde –

<u>Meeting the Billionaire Boss – In the Name of Love Book 1</u>
Edward Cavendish: Losing my wife two years ago was not something anyone expected. Lucille was beautiful and successful, and I thought we'd spend our lives together. Turns out I was wrong. Facing the world feels impossible so I shut myself away in my mansion in the countryside where only my young son can bring a smile to my face.

Ava Thorne: I'm broke. More than broke, actually. I have mountains of debt and it's getting worse by the day. I've been working two jobs to support my sick mother and younger brother, but when I'm fired from the one over a mistake that wasn't mine, I don't know where to turn.

Edward: My son's nanny is going away on the trip of a lifetime, so I need to find a replacement. It has to be someone we can trust but the thought of having anyone else in my home turns me cold. Plus, there's the inheritance clause that states I must be

Also from Wynter Wilde –

married on my 35th birthday and the date looms ever closer...

Ava: When the opportunity of a lifetime arises in the chance to earn a large sum of money fast, I'm forced to confront my past and decide if I can embrace a future I never dreamt of.

And it all starts with meeting the billionaire boss...

Healing the Billionaire's Heart – In the Name of Love Book 2

Jack Kendrick: These days, I guess I'm what they refer to as a sworn bachelor. Finding my teenage sweetheart in bed with my so-called best friend led me to rule out relationships. There's no way any woman is ever going to hurt me like that again. All I want to focus on is building my business empire and having a good time.

Grace Cosgrove: As wedding planner, you'd think I'd love weddings. I used to, until my mogul fiancé dumped me at the altar. Every wedding I plan breaks my heart a little bit more and I don't think I'll ever feel joy in my job or my non-existent romantic life again.

Jack: There's a wedding on the horizon and as best man, I have to get involved. I'm not overjoyed at the prospect but when I see the wedding planner... well... sparks fly in more ways than one. The groom tells me I'd better leave her alone, but I find her simply irresistible.

Grace: This could be the wedding of the year, a real-life Cinderella story, and they've chosen me to plan the wedding. It's brilliant for business, but it

Also from Wynter Wilde –

also means I have to summon some enthusiasm. Then I meet the best man and I wish he'd stop looking at me like that because I'm struggling to focus as it is.

Will Grace heal Jack's heart, or will they go their separate ways before the wedding speeches are done?

About the Author

Wynter Wilde writes passionate and emotional romances featuring brooding heroes and strong heroines.

Connect with her on:

Printed in Great Britain
by Amazon